Comic Sense

by Nancy Mucklow

illustrations by Nancy Mucklow

Comic Sense

 Michael Grass House
Kingston, Ontario Canada K7M2W2

Copyright © 2010 by Nancy Mucklow
Cover design by Belinda McGee
Illustrations by Nancy Mucklow

All rights reserved, including the right of reproduction in whole or in part in any form.

The information in this book is true and complete to the best of our knowledge.
Comic Sense is not intended to replace professional occupational therapy or professional diagnosis or advice. The contents are not medical, legal, technical, or therapeutic advice and must not be construed as such. Readers should not use this information to diagnose or treat social communication disabilities without consulting a qualified professional. All descriptions, recommendations, and activity suggestions are made without guarantee on the part of the author. The author disclaims any liability in connection with the use of this information.

ISBN - 978-0-9811439-5-8   1. Social skills training 2. ADHD, treatments 3. Asperger syndrome, treatments

CONTENTS

What is Common Sense? 7
    Being aware 9
    Predicting 12
    Knowing what people assume and expect 16
    Prioritizing 20
    Knowing what to do 22
    Asking for help 27

1 Context 29
    Place 33
    Time 35
    Situation 39
    People 41

2 Perspective 51
    The context lens 54
    The experience lens 55
    The strangeness lens 57
    The why lens 60
    The trust lens 61
    The priority lens 63
    The friend lens 65

3 Personal Perspectives 67
    Wants, needs, and feelings 69
    Memories and experiences 73
    Facts and information 74
    Personal mirrors 77
    Different kinds of normal 80
    The need to form conclusions 82
    Manners and social rules 86
    Tact 88

4 Safety 97
Safety as a flashlight 99
Safety and people 100
Safety and context 102
Safety and perspective 106
Safety and personal perspective 108
Safety and personal mirrors 112
Safety and impulsivity 115
Safety and fear 116

5 Relationships 121
Deposits in a relationship 123
Wants, needs, and expectations 132
Close friendships 134
Groups 138
Solving relationship problems 142

6 Communication 149
Body language and voice 152
A smile as a message 158
Silence as a message 159
Eye connection 161
People reading you 163
First impressions 167

7 Conversation 171
Conversation and people 173
Conversation and equality 174
Conversation and personal perspectives 177
Group conversations 182
Four unwritten rules of conversation 188
Repairing conversations 192
Having a sense of humor 196
Personal space 202

Suggested Answers to Quiz Boxes 205

If common sense is so common, then why don't I have it?

Common sense isn't something you are born with. It's something that you learn.

If you...

- *often get told that you don't have common sense,*
- *bump into invisible problems,*
- *lose friends and make people angry for reasons you don't understand,*
- *feel frustrated in social situations because you're the only person who doesn't know what's going on,*
- *are constantly surprised at what people expect you to know without someone telling you,*
- *find that the social skills you learn in books usually work only in books, and*
- *sometimes feel like an alien from another planet,*

...then this book is for you.

This book will show you what common sense is. There are cartoons and diagrams to help you visualize the concepts, and comics to show you how they work.

Of course, the phrase *common sense* has many different meanings. Some people think it means proverbs; others think it means traditional ideas. In this book, *common sense* means only one thing: the kind of practical thinking skills that most people develop early in life and that keep them out of trouble for the rest of their lives.

So rather than giving a list of common sense ideas, this book will help you learn to become *commonly sensible*.

Comic Sense is not a social skills book. But if you figure out how to think with common sense, you'll find social skills much easier to learn and much more natural to use.

INTRODUCTION
What is Common Sense?

There was only one thought on Jennie's mind that morning: her college entrance exams. She shifted impatiently from one foot to another as the bus crawled toward her school. When her bus finally reached her stop, she leaped out the door and dashed across the street.

The sudden screech of tires almost stopped her breathing. A car had braked just inches from her.

"Don't you have any common sense?" the driver yelled. "You're going to get killed!"

Her heart pounding, Jennie couldn't move. "Get out of the way!" the driver howled. "Don't just stand there!"

"Sorry!" Jennie escaped to the side of the road as the car squealed past her. Panting, she tried to focus her thoughts. "I don't even know what happened," she moaned to herself.

What is common sense?

If you've been told you don't have common sense, then you might be wondering what it is. A lot of people use the term without being able to explain it.

Common sense is...

- **reasoning skills** that you can adapt to any situation
- **the ability to think quickly**, followed by quick action
- **instincts**, practical knowledge, and awareness of human nature

Common sense is not...

- **rules to memorize:** You can't memorize common sense, just as you can't memorize how to swim.
- **intelligence:** Common sense won't help you write a novel or design a skyscraper.
- **political ideas:** Politicians like to use the term "common sense" to insult their opponents. But political ideas are too complex to be common sense.

People learn common sense very slowly throughout their entire lives. Babies learn simple things: *If you drop something, no matter how many times, it always falls to the floor. If you smile at someone, they smile back.* Children learn more advanced things: *If you share with a friend, that friend might share back some day. If you eat too much candy, you get a sore stomach.*

By the time people reach adulthood, they've learned the basics of common sense. For the rest of their lives, they simply add to it.

There are very few people who have no common sense. Most people have some common sense about certain things, but they may have holes in their knowledge.

If this is you, then the first step is figuring out what common sense is.

Common sense is about

- **awareness**
- **predictability**
- **other people's assumptions and expectations**
- **prioritizing**
- **knowing what to do**
- **asking for help**

1. Being aware

Common sense starts with awareness. When you are aware, you can see what is going on around you. When you're not aware, then you won't see what's going on around you. Awareness means paying attention, with your eyes and mind open and alert.

Children develop common sense by being aware of adults. Over time, they learn by correcting their mistakes and asking questions. By the time they are adults, most people have all the basic common sense skills they need.

But some children find it hard to be aware. Their brains aren't naturally tuned in to people and surroundings. Some aren't even aware that they aren't aware! These children often don't learn common sense. As adults, they struggle to figure out what is going on.

Staying aware is a particular challenge for people with ADHD and Asperger Syndrome.

What to do

The next time someone says, "That's just common sense!" ask them what they mean.

Is it science? Is it fact?

Is it instinct?

Is it reasoning skills?

Or is it opinions and complex ideas?

Or rules?

Or knowledge that comes from a book?

Bubble mind

Some people have a mind that is like a bubble. They like to think about their own thoughts and ideas. But they have a hard time focusing on the outer world and usually don't observe enough to figure out what other people are thinking.

Jake is creative. He's always thinking up new ideas for creative projects. Today he has been thinking about a video he wants to make. He missed his bus this morning because he was looking up information about video formats on the internet instead of getting ready for the day. He also forgot his history assignment at home.

He wasn't really listening all day, so he's now not sure what he's supposed to have done for tomorrow.

Do You Have a Bubble Mind?

_____ I have special interests that I like to think about all the time. Sometimes this gets in the way of doing other things.

_____ I get startled when people stop me and tell me what I've done something wrong. It's always a shock.

_____ I often forget things because I'm thinking about something else.

_____ I can focus on one activity for hours if it really interests me.

Hummingbird mind

Some people have a mind like a hummingbird. It flies from one exciting idea to the next, without staying long enough to learn anything. They have a hard time focusing on what other people are saying or doing.

What Is Common Sense?

Mia is late... again. This morning was a typical morning. While getting ready for the day, she finished a crossword puzzle, checked her email, chose what she would wear on the weekend, and sorted her sock drawer. And then, suddenly, it was time to catch the bus!

Where did the time go? And she hadn't even made her lunch or gotten dressed yet.

Do You Have a Hummingbird Mind?

_____ I get really excited about new ideas and activities—so excited that I don't pay attention to what I'm doing.

_____ I find so many things interesting! My attention goes from one great idea to the next.

_____ When I have a great new idea, I forget about other people and what they want.

_____ I can't focus on anything for very long. My mind is always moving on to something else.

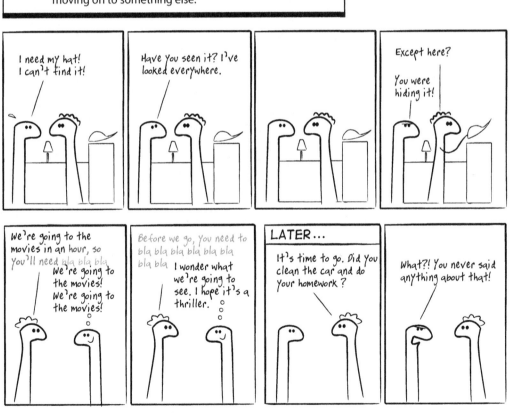

What to do if you aren't very aware

Everybody is a little bit unaware. But if you find it hard to stay aware for every long, then you might need some help.

Three kinds of treatments are available: medications, neurofeedback, and meditation. Each one works in its own way. But many people manage to teach themselves to be more aware through counselling, special programs, and mental discipline.

If you have awareness problems, you will probably always have them in some form or another all your life. But you can still learn about common sense and use it whenever your awareness kicks in.

2. Predicting

Being able to predict what's going to happen is part of common sense. If you are aware what's going on around you, then you'll have a good idea what's coming.

Of course, nobody can predict the whole future. Common sense is not a crystal ball. But you can predict anything that's predictable.

So then how do you know what's predictable? Start by becoming aware that the world follows *patterns*.

A world of patterns

If you believe that everything is random and that things just happen, then you won't realize what's predictable.

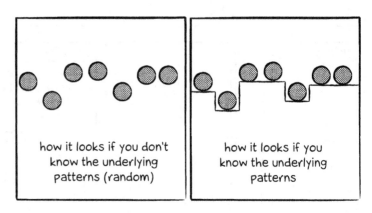

The truth is that most things in life are not random. If you stopped to think, you'd realize that events that happen to you are not entirely unpredictable.

- You are carrying a huge pile of books. One slips from your grasp, and the whole pile topples to the floor. Is this a random event, or was it predictable?

- You are running frantically to catch the bus. Then you trip over a ridge in the sidewalk and fall. Is this a random event, or was it predictable?

- You see a crowd of people screaming and running out of a building. Should you conclude they're behaving randomly, or is there probably a reason for their actions?

Here are the ideas behind common-sense predictions:

- **Nothing is random:** Everything happens for a reason. The reason might be hard to figure out, or it might just be a feeling or impulse, but there is a reason.

- **Everything follows patterns:** Things tend to happen the same way over and over again. If you've seen it happen that way once, and if nothing changes, it will probably happen that way again.

- **Patterns are predictable:** If you know the reasons why things are happening, and you've observed the patterns, you can predict what will happen next. You'll feel in control of the situation and confident that you're prepared for what's coming.

One man was fidgeting in the line-up at Lena's service desk. He was shifting from one foot to another, exhaling very loudly and pressing his lips tight. Then he'd roll his eyes, look around, then glare at her.

She asked him why he was fidgeting. The man said very curtly, "No reason."

Lena decided that his behavior was completely random and just ignored it. Instead, she concentrated on getting her work done.

But later, she learned that the man went on to file a complaint about her poor service. He was angry about how long it had taken for her to process his papers. And he was even more angry because Lena had ignored him!

Had she thought about his behavior, instead of assuming it was random, she might have realized he was trying to show her that he was angry about the wait. She would have been able to explain the process to him and help him out.

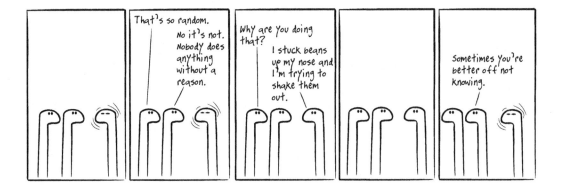

Science and nature patterns

The laws of science and nature are patterns. Once you know these patterns, you can predict what will happen.

Examples:

- **Gravity:** *Things fall. Often they break when they hit the ground.*
- **Speed and inertia:** *Things moving fast will continue to move fast unless something powerful stops them.*
- **Biology:** *Wet and warm conditions make things grow (like bacteria and mold).*
- **Electricity:** *Household electricity is powerful enough to kill a person.*

Social patterns

Because people live together, they follow social patterns. If people didn't, then they would always be insulting, inconveniencing, and hurting others.

Examples:

- **How to have a conversation:** *People follow patterns of politeness, listening, talking, and being pleasant. They follow different patterns depending how well they know the people they're talking to.*

- **How to eat with people:** *People use standard table manners when eating with others. They adapt those manners depending on where they are eating.*
- **How to get to know someone:** *People use standard introductions and get-to-know-you patterns when meeting new people.*

Predicting with Patterns

Situation	Pattern	Prediction
A tower of stacked boxes seems unbalanced.	Gravity pulls things down.	If no one balances this stack of boxes, it will fall over.
The freezer door is open.	Cold air falls out of an open freezer, and moist warm air goes in.	If no one closes the freezer, the food will thaw.
I would like the last piece of pie.	Polite people always ask if someone else wants the last treat before they take it.	If I don't ask first, then people will think I'm impolite.
I am driving, and I want to turn left.	Drivers must signal and wait for the other lane to clear before they turn left.	If I don't signal and wait for the other lane to clear, _____
I forgot to feed the cat today.	_____	_____

See page 205 for suggested answers to quiz boxes.

You can predict

1. **Events are rarely completely random.**
   Everything has a reason, even if you don't know what it is.
2. **Objects follow the patterns of science and nature.**
   If you learn basic science, you can have common sense.
3. **People follow social patterns.**
   Social patterns adapt to each situation.

3. Knowing what people assume and expect

One of the hardest parts of common sense is knowing what other people think. Sure, you can't see inside their heads. But with a little work, you can figure out what they're probably thinking.

Examples of assumptions:

- Your work partner notices that you haven't done your share of the work. He assumes that you are selfish, you don't care about his time, and you expect him to do all the work.

- You and your girlfriend have an argument, and then you forget to call her for two days. She assumes that you are ignoring her deliberately because you are still angry about the argument.

- You borrow things and then return them broken. People assume you are careless and don't respect their things. They also assume you don't care about your friendship with them.

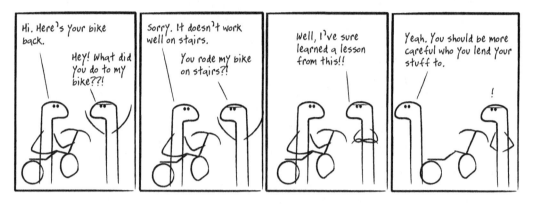

Examples of expectations:

- You are watching a play in a small theatre with some of your friends. Your friends and everyone else in the audience expect you to sit still, stay quiet, and watch the production.

- You are walking up to the edge of a road to cross the street. The drivers on that road all expect you to look up and check the traffic before you step out onto the road.

- You were supposed to call your boyfriend this morning, but you forgot. When you see your boyfriend, he expects you to explain what happened.

Figuring Out Expectations

Situation	Expectation
I am at a party at my friend's house.	My friend expects me to be friendly and outgoing, and not to be too serious.
I am driving, and I move into the left-turn lane.	Other drivers expect me to turn left.
My young cousin, who is three years old, has fallen and hurt herself.	She expects me to run over and help her because I am her big cousin.
I open a large bag of chips while sitting with my friends in the cafeteria.	My friends expect me to _____
I borrow my friend's bike.	She expects me to _____
My teammate throws the ball to me while I'm running, but he throws it ahead of me.	He expects me to _____

"Nobody will mind"

Don't assume that nobody will care if you do something outside of the social patterns. They *will* care—a lot. But according to social rules, they're not supposed to tell you that you've broken a rule. It's consider rude to correct someone.

They also assume you know the patterns, so they conclude you are doing it wrong on purpose, just to annoy or inconvenience them.

So just because they don't say anything, that doesn't mean they don't mind. They are too polite to tell you.

People expect

...that you know the social patterns

If you break them without explaining why, they assume you did it on purpose.

What Is Common Sense?

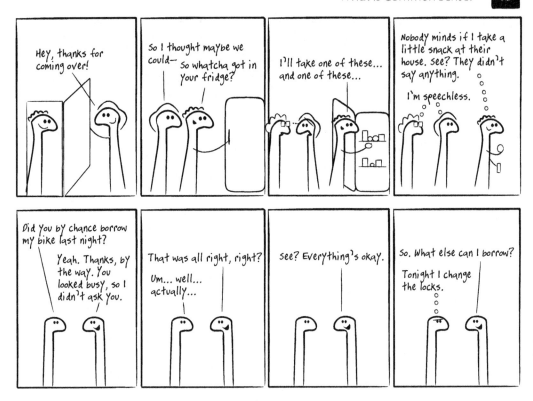

Xiang's first staff meeting was going to be a big success.

Sure, she ended up arriving 10 minutes late, but it was no big deal. Then she accidentally let the door slam, but she apologized right away.

She was also chewing gum, because nobody said she couldn't, and she popped a few bubbles while she listened. Her friend Lynn frowned and whispered at her to be quiet.

Xiang didn't know what Lynn's problem was, because nobody else was complaining. Xiang assumed that meant nobody minded.

But she wasn't really looking to see if they did mind. If she had, she would have noticed the glares and frowns. She also didn't consider their expectations. They would expect her to be quiet and attentive and willing to learn, especially since she was a new employee.

The boss had expectations of her own. The next day, Xiang got called into the boss's office for a "talk."

4. Prioritizing

What's more important: to avoid being late, or to do the job well? The answer is *It depends*. If missing the deadline means your company loses the contract, then the priority is to meet the deadline. But if the work will be worthless unless it's complete and thorough, then your priority is to do the job well. You can always ask for an extension.

Prioritizing means deciding what's more important in the situation and then doing things in the right order.

Ana runs every night after dark.
Tonight her friend Carlos is running with her.

As she is coming up to a driveway, she notices a car with its headlights on and its motor running. She realizes that the driver is about to back out of the driveway, so she sprints to get past.

But she trips and falls, scraping her knee badly. Groaning, she tries to sit up. Just then, Carlos grabs her and drags her across the gritty asphalt onto the grass—just as the car started to back up.

"Ouch! What are you doing?" Ana cries out angrily, wincing at the pain.

"Saving your life!" Carlos yells back. "What were you doing just lying there? Why didn't you roll out of the way?"

Ana looks around, confused. Her only answer is that she didn't think of it.

Tips for prioritizing:

- **Be aware that some things are more important than others:** Everything may seem equally urgent, until you think it through. A scraped knee, no matter how painful, is a lot less important than a car backing up where you are sitting.

- **Use the inverted triangle method:** Practice thinking about activities and problems in an inverted triangle. The ones with the biggest consequences go in the wider part, and the ones with the smallest consequences go lower down.

You can prioritize

1. **Things that cause death**
   ...come before...
2. **Things that cause injury**
   ...which come before...
3. **Things that cause problems**
   ...such as lateness, inconvenience, or costs.

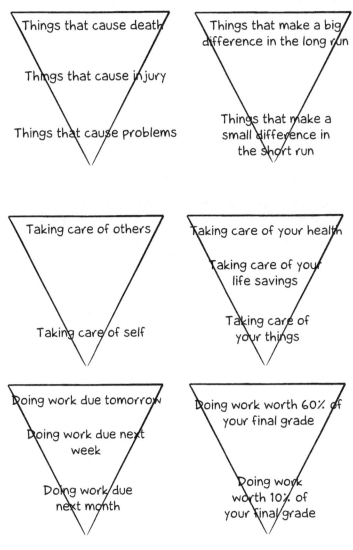

When facing choices, imagine the priority triangle. Decide which choice is most important and rank them downward. Then tackle the highest-priority item first.

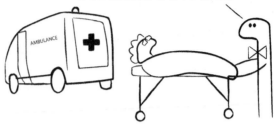

 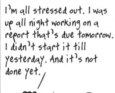 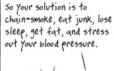 

What's Higher Priority? Rank 1–4

_____ If I don't shoot any moose, I will have wasted the money on a hunting permit.

_____ If I forget to put the hunting rifle away, a child might accidently shoot someone with it.

_____ If I don't buy lots of ammunition, I probably won't have extra in case we decide to hunt the next day.

_____ If I don't take the time to clean the rifle, my father will be furious with me and won't let me use it again.

5. Knowing what to do

When people talk about common sense, they also mean that they expect you to know what to do, which usually means:

- *solving the problem*
- *cleaning up the mess*
- *taking responsibility*
- *avoiding predictable problems*
- *adapting to the patterns*

When you can't think

Sometimes the problem is that you can't think. You know you have to do something, but your brain can't focus on it.

People blame you for not reacting, but the truth is that you weren't able to do anything. Your brain simply wasn't working.

There are several different reasons why your brain can stop working.

1. Brain freeze

> **Jessica was starving.** She'd been working on her website for hours, forgetting about everything else, and now all she could think about was grabbing something to eat.
>
> She ran over to the fridge and pulled out some cold pizza and juice. She poured herself a quick glass and swung around to put the juice carton back in the fridge.
>
> But because she was moving so fast, the carton slipped from her hand. Suddenly there was juice everywhere, in the fridge, on the floor, on her clothes!
>
> Jessica stood frozen for a long second, unable to move. She stared at the mess. Even speaking was hard. She tried to say something or call out for help, but all that came out was a yelp.
>
> Finally, she screamed. Her roommate Lisa came rushing over. "It's only spilled juice," Lisa said, annoyed. "Just wipe it up."
>
> "Uh... what... I don't know what to do...!" Jessica cried. She stared at the mess, feeling panic bubbling up inside.

A brain freeze occurs when you get shocked, disoriented, or angry. Something surprises you by spilling, not working, or interrupting what you're doing. Suddenly there is so much confusion in your brain that you can't think.

Do You Get Brain Freezes?

_____	I panic when something unexpectedly goes wrong.
_____	Interruptions always come like big shocks. They jolt me, and then I can't think properly.
_____	When a problem suddenly comes up, unless I've seen that problem before, I have no idea what to do.
_____	When I get angry, I can't think. I usually yell, pound things, and just get angrier.

What to do

1. **Take a step back.**
   Problems look smaller from farther back.

2. **Take a deep breath.**
   Breathing will help you calm down.

3. **Talk to yourself.**
   Tell your brain what it needs to know.

Tips for brain freezes

A brain freeze happens because too much emotion suddenly clogs your brain. You need to unclog it before you'll be able to think.

- **Take a step back:** Look at the situation from a few steps away so that the problem doesn't look as big. You'll also be able to see the situation the way other people see it. Even the simple action of backing up may help unfreeze your brain.

- **Take a deep breath:** Breathing slowly helps get rid of panicky feelings. It replaces strong emotions like fear and surprise with soothing emotions. It also helps your body relax. One deep breath might be enough to unfreeze your brain.

- **Talk to yourself:** Tell yourself out loud what happened. Describe the problem. When your brain hears your words, it may start thinking again.

2. Impulsivity

Tony and his buddies were playing little practical jokes on each other all day. Things got kind of silly. Tony felt wild and excited, jumping from one prank and one idea to another.

Then Tony had the great idea of setting a large plastic bucket of water on top of Kenny's door. When Kenny opened the door, he'd get water on his head. Giddily, Tony set it all up.

But when Kenny opened the door, the bucket crashed down hard on his head. Kenny was knocked unconscious. Tony stood there, not knowing what to do, as the others ran around doing first aid and calling an ambulance.

Tony was completely confused. What happened? How did he not realize that the bucket could hurt his friend?

Impulsivity means being swept away by fun, excitement, and cool ideas that overcome good sense. It means acting without thinking. Afterward, you realize what you did wrong. But at the time, your brain was so full of excitement and energy that you couldn't think.

What Is Common Sense?

Are You Impulsive?

_____ People tell me I act without thinking.

_____ I feel excitement very strongly—so strongly that I usually can't think of anything else.

_____ I find everything interesting. I'm curious about everything I see or hear.

_____ I often don't finish what I start. I'm usually onto the next project before the first one is done.

Tips for impulsivity

There are lots of treatments for impulsivity, so you may want to consult a doctor or psychologist to learn about your options. But here are some basic tips for dealing with impulsive moments.

- **Learn the signs:** What does impulsivity feel like to you? Does it feel like a motor running too fast? Do you breathe quickly? Do you feel hot? Do people have a way of looking at you or talking to you when you are impulsive? When you know the signs, you can figure out when you are impulsive, before it gets you into trouble.

- **Keep fit and healthy:** People who eat a good diet, get lots of exercise, and sleep eight hours a night are better at controlling impulsivity than people who are unhealthy.

- **Designate an impulsivity buddy:** Ask a close friend be your impulsivity buddy. Allow this friend to talk to you and get you out of the situation when he/she sees you starting to lose control.

What to do

1. **Learn to recognize the signs.**
   Prevent impulsivity by stopping it before it gets out of control.

2. **Get lots of sleep, exercise, and healthy food.**
   Healthy habits keep your body calm and content.

3. **Get an impulsivity buddy.**
   This friend takes you aside when you are getting out of control.

3. Preocccupation

Joe loves trains. He has a miniature model railway set up in his parent's basement. He spent the day working on upgrading the scenery and expanding the track while his parents were out.

Suddenly, the phone rang, piercing his concentration. Joe roared with exasperation. Just when he was about to test the train in the new tunnel!

He answered the phone, still thinking about the tunnel. Will it work? Is it tall enough?

The call was for his father. "Yes... mm-hm...," he murmured as the caller rattled off some information. But his agitation was growing. "Okay... okay... I'll give him the message. All right?" Relieved, he slammed down the phone and rushed back to his project.

When his parents got home, he had long forgotten about the call. Since he wasn't thinking enough to write down the message, his father didn't get the information.

Preoccupation means thinking about a favorite interest, daydreaming, or obsessing. Preoccupation isn't a problem until you need to turn your attention to something important and take some action. When you are preoccupied, you may not even realize that you aren't thinking. You don't usually realize it until a long time later. By that time, it's too late.

Do You Get Preoccupied?

_____ I daydream a lot. I think about the things I want to do instead of what I'm supposed to be doing.

_____ Often when people tell me things, a few minutes later I can't remember anything they said.

_____ When I'm out walking, I'm always thinking about something. I don't notice where I'm walking.

_____ When I have a good idea, I want to think about it. I don't want people to talk to me till I'm done thinking.

Tips for preoccupation

Being able to concentrate is a good thing. The only problem is being unable to switch your attention to something else when you need to.

- **Take breaks:** Every now and then, interrupt your concentration. Stretch, stand up, look around the room, or have a snack. This helps prevent your brain from getting stuck.

> **What to do**
>
> **Take breaks.**
> *Let your brain have a rest from thinking about one thing.*

How to know what to do

How can you know the right action to take? That is a topic we will cover in the main chapters of this book. For now, keep in mind that common sense is usually very simple:

- *If you make a mess, you clean it up.*
- *If you break something, you fix it.*
- *If you have gone too far, you back up.*
- *If you feel sick, you go to bed.*
- *If you are lost, you find someone or something to guide you.*
- *If don't like where you're going, change where you're headed.*

6. Asking for help

Finally, common sense means knowing when you don't know what to do. That's when you need help from someone else.

There's nothing wrong with asking for help. It doesn't mean you're unintelligent or helpless. It means that you *know* when you *don't know* something, which is pretty smart.

It's better to get help and do things right than to do them wrong.

Rae started to wonder if she had taken the wrong road.

She pulled over and looked at the instructions again. Her boss had written them up for her, but he might have left something out.

Should she just keep driving? After all, she was following what he'd written.

Rae decided that option didn't make sense. She knew that she didn't know where she was. Getting more lost wouldn't help.

She parked the car and went into a store to ask for directions.

Summary

Common sense is a practical way of thinking. It's not memorized rules, popular ideas, or intelligence; it's reasoning skills, quick-thinking skills, and instincts.

It also includes

- **being aware:** Common sense means knowing what's happening around you.
- **being able to predict:** Common sense means learning to predict everything that is predictable. Never assume that anything is random.
- **knowing what other people assume or expect:** Common sense means seeing social patterns people use and being aware when you aren't following them.
- **prioritizing**: Common sense means knowing what's more important.
- **learning to think and act:** Common sense means teaching your brain to work all the time.
- **asking for help:** Common sense means avoiding mistakes is better than trying to look as if you know what you're doing.

So that's what common sense *is*. Now we can look at how it works and what you can do about it.

Chapter 1
Context

Louise arrived at Kate's party early.

Just in case it was a dull party, she'd brought along a book.

Kate frowned at the sight of the book as she took Louise's coat. "What's that for?"

"In case I can't find anything to do," Louise answered.

"A book might be okay for class, but it's not okay for a party," Kate said, looking worried. "I don't want my party wrecked by someone reading. Talk to people, and don't be serious!"

So Louise found Ron and chatted with him for a while. He told her he was going into surgery in the morning. She laughed and made some light jokes. He looked surprised and suddenly excused himself and left.

She found some other friends and joked around with them. Later, Louise walked home with them. She kept up the jokes.

"Hey!" one girl said suddenly, grabbing her jacket. "Watch out! You almost walked out into traffic. You know, maybe you should talk a little less and start focusing on where you are!"

What is context?

Context is what you are in. Your context can be the place you are in. But it can also be the time (there are good times and bad times for doing things). It can also be the situation or circumstances—the details of what's happening around you. As well, the context can be the people nearby.

Each of these context factors change what you should do, how you should do it, and other similar decisions.

The thing to remember about context is *Not here*, *Not now*, *Not when this is going on*, and *Not when these people are around*. The context affects what actions are okay or not okay, so you have to be aware of context to act appropriately.

Fitting things into contexts

You can think of context like this sorting puzzle. The eleven objects can fit into both of the contexts (the square and the triangle). But you have to arrange them differently to fit the shape of each context.

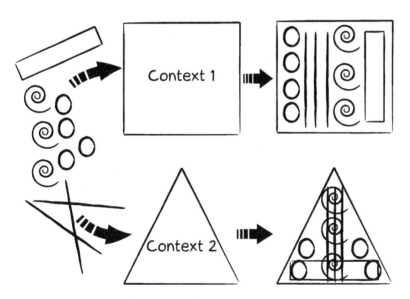

Things you say and do are like the eleven objects: you have to make sure they fit in the context. If you don't fit, they'll stick out—cause problems, make people angry, or disrupt what's going on.

Context is like a party invitation

Context is like an invitation because both focus on place, time, situation, and people. The information in an invitation gives you an idea what patterns are going to be expected at that party.

Invitation

The Ladies' Muffin Club Annual Poetry Reading Recital

Date: Tuesday 7:00 till 9:00 p.m.

Location: Country Club Salon

Featured Guest: Miss Maybeline Marberry, Poetry Recital Queen

Tea, coffee, and muffins will be served.

Yer invited!

Date: Sat'day, mid'night til we're done wi' yer

Place: The Vengeful Maid Pirate Ship, anchor'd in Blackbeard Bay

For to git to know th' locals heh heh heh heh heh

Show up or we'll come 'n get yer!

Before you go to the party, you probably ask yourself about the social patterns and expectations:

> How should I dress?
>
> Should I bring any food or drink?
>
> Should I ask someone to go with me as a date? Should I go with a group?
>
> What kind of party is it? Should I call and ask?
>
> When I'm there, how much should I eat or drink?
>
> Is this a formal event or just a casual party? Should I use casual manners or formal manners?
>
> How loud will the party be? Will there be music and dancing?
>
> Will I know anybody there?
>
> What's the right way to handle this invitation?

Like an invitation, context gives you an idea what people expect for that event. People have expectations based on the place, the time, the situation, and, of course, themselves and any other people nearby.

People assume

... you will assess an event before you go.
Because they always do.

People expect

... you will fit your actions to the patterns of the events.
Because it's considerate of others.

1. Place

Many social patterns have to do with the place you are in. People have different expectations, based on the place, about how you will act.

The purpose of the place

What people expect depends on the *purpose* of the place. When you know the purpose, you can figure out what people expect you to do. For example, the purpose of a ballpark is playing and having fun. The purpose of a railway station is getting on or off trains.

Avoid doing anything that gets in the way of the purpose of a place. If the purpose is to have fun, then avoid being a downer. If the purpose is to learn, then be attentive and avoid being disruptive. If the purpose is to listen, then avoid talking.

Purpose and Expectations of a Place		
Place	**Purpose**	**What not to do**
road	to move (safely)	Don't do anything that obstructs traffic or breaks safety rules.
restaurant	to eat (and socialize)	Don't do anything that causes people to lose their appetite or ruins the fun atmosphere.
party	to be social (and fun)	Don't read, ignore people, or talk about solemn topics.
job interview	to impress a boss (and get a job offer)	Don't do anything that is flippant or disrespectful.
funeral	to _____	_____

How do you figure out the purpose of a place? You take the time to observe and think before you jump in.

The 10-second room zoom

Most people look around and size up a place before they walk in. They figure out the purpose and expectations first. You can do this too.

- Before entering a new place (or an event in a new place), stand near the doorway, but not in the way of people using the doorway.
- Observe the room for 10 seconds. How is the room arranged? Who is here? What are they doing? How loud or quiet is the room? You are looking for patterns.
- Figure out the purpose of the place (or event).
- Decide what people expect you to do and not to do, based on the purpose.
- Enter the place, and match your actions to the patterns you observed.

What to do

1. **Observe the place.**
   Do a 10-second room zoom.
2. **Identify the purpose.**
   There may be more than one.
3. **Decide what people expect from you.**
   Expectations are based on the purpose.
4. **Match the purpose and expectations.**
   Follow the expected patterns.

It was Cara's first house concert, and she didn't know what to expect.

So she zoomed the room as soon as she arrived. She noticed that the chairs were arranged in rows in a semi-circle and that there were glasses of water on a table beside two of the chairs. She wondered why two people had water glasses but nobody else. Then she realized that those chairs were reserved for the singers.

She also noticed that there were programs and jackets on chairs in the front row. She decided to move them, because that's where she wanted to sit. Then she heard someone say,

"Save me a seat, too!" She watched a man put his jacket and hat on two more chairs. She realized that people were using jackets and programs to save seats.

Finally, she looked at the people. Most were standing at the back of the room in small groups talking to each other. She noticed a friend of hers, so she went over to talk to her.

2. Time

Have you ever been told you have a good sense of timing or a bad sense of timing? Time is part of context, just like place. For any moment in time, there are events that came before it and events that are coming after it—and other events that are occurring at the same time. Each part of the time context affects what you should or shouldn't do.

Events that have already happened affect what's okay to do right now. If someone just spilled gasoline, then it's not okay to light a match. If your friend was sick yesterday, it's not okay to complain about her work not being done.

Events that are about to happen also affect what's okay right now. If an electrical storm is in the forecast, it's not okay go out boating now. If visitors are due to arrive tomorrow, it's not okay to mess up the house now.

If you are aware of what came before and what's coming after, you will understand what's appropriate for right now.

People assume

... you remember the past and consider how it affects the present.
Because they do.

People expect

... you will make logical predictions about what will happen in the near future.
And take action.

What happened BEFORE?

- Yesterday?
- An hour ago?
- Five minutes ago?
- Last year at this time?
- Could any of these events affect what is appropriate right now?

What will happen AFTER?

- Tomorrow?
- In an hour?
- Five minutes from now?
- A year from today?
- Could any of these events affect what is appropriate right now?

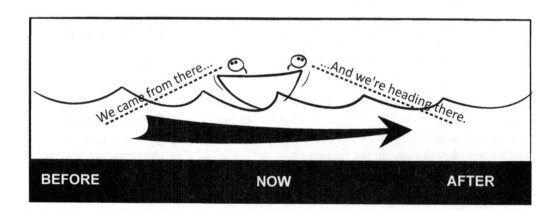

Good timing is essential in sports.

To be a good player, you have to keep in mind what's already happened. How many times has each player scored? How fast has each player been running? What techniques has each player used? You use this information to decide what's the right strategy for right now.

More important, you have to think about what's about to happen. If Player 1 is running toward you at a fast speed, and Player 2 is running behind you at a moderate speed, where will they both be when you catch the ball? Will they be able to grab it from you?

And if you decide to pass that ball, you'll have to consider where your teammate will be by the time the ball flies through the air. If she's running, you'll have to throw it to where she'll be in a few seconds, not to where she is right now.

Events coming BEFORE can...

- **make ordinary actions dangerous:** *Yesterday, Cam's dog chewed up the lamp cord. Today, plugging it in would be a hazard.*

- **make a person feel upset:** *John learned ten minutes ago that he failed his driver's test. Now he is not in the mood to joke around with you.*

- **leave a person scared:** *Saul was robbed last night at gunpoint. Now he is afraid to walk out at night, even to go to a movie he wants to see.*

- **affect a person's confidence:** *Leila won the Employee of the Year award yesterday. Now she's in a terrific mood. This might be a good time to ask for funding for your new project idea.*

You can predict

1. **Consider what happened earlier.**
   Does anything in the past affect what's right or wrong right now?

2. **Consider what's going to happen soon.**
   Remember: that's where you're headed.

3. **Predict what could go wrong if you ignore these**
   Choose actions that flow from past events and prepare for future events.

Events coming AFTER can...

- **make actions necessary:** *Sometime tomorrow, a hurricane will roll ashore. Now is the time to board up the windows.*

- **make a person feel worried:** *Ron has his driver's exam in 20 minutes. Now he is not in the mood to joke around.*

- **make a person sensitive:** *Betta has to perform her song next week. Now she is extremely upset by every tiny mistake she makes.*

- **make a person tense:** *Sam has to ask the boss for a raise later today. Now he can't focus on the conversation.*

Predictions for Good Timing

Before	Now	Future
Ten minutes ago, I saw the electrical outlet giving off sparks.	I want to plug in the blender.	I might blow a fuse. I might get a bad shock. I shouldn't plug it in (unless I repair the outlet).
I heard that yesterday, my friend Sam was really sick with the flu.	I want to ask Sam to enter the hotdog-eating contest with me today.	

Now	After	Future
I want to go on a long hike today.	A heat wave is supposed to arrive this afternoon.	I might get heat exhaustion. I shouldn't go on the hike (or I should go on a shorter hike).
I am telling Louise a long story.	Louise has to meet her boyfriend downtown in five minutes.	

3. Situation

Situation refers to all the details and circumstances that make one place and time different from another.

For example, if you always play soccer in the park at 3:00 p.m. on Monday, then the place and time are pretty much always the same. But last Monday, it was hot, and there was a big crowd of spectators because it happened to be a holiday; this Monday, it's pouring rain, and the bleachers are empty. Last Monday, a construction crew was blowing up sand and dust; this Monday, the field is drenched and too slippery for running.

When the circumstances change, what's okay or not okay changes too. Common sense means adapting to the reality of the situation, not to what it used to be or what you think it should be.

Enoch has to make an oral presentation about drug safety.

He was planning to start with a few jokes to catch everyone's attention. But today a student was taken from school in an ambulance, and the rumor is that he had overdosed on a prescription medicine. Enoch knows that his audience is now thinking about that student. They won't enjoy the jokes.

The situation has changed. Enoch now has to adapt his presentation to the new situation.

So he decides to start his talk with some information about recent improvements in treatment for drug overdoses instead of the jokes.

Adapting to changing situations

Unlike place and time, situations can change quickly. When circumstances change, they often change the purpose of the place. For example, you go to a friend's house to play cards; but when you arrive, your friend tells you the house just got broken into. The circumstances of your visit have now changed. You'll be helping to deal with the emergency, not playing cards.

Common sense means that when important details about the situation change, you change your actions to match.

People assume

... you are aware of changing circumstances.
These details often change the purpose of the place.

People expect

... you will change your actions to fit the new situation.
Problems will occur if you don't.

Adapting to the Situation		
Normal	**Change**	**Adaptation**
I walk to school along this road every day.	Today, police cars and fire trucks have blocked off the road.	I will take a different route. I won't try to walk through the emergency area in case it's dangerous.
I always hang my jacket in the closet.	My jacket is soaking wet today because it's raining.	

Adapting to change can be difficult if you like following routines. It's even harder if you hate change or find it disorienting.

The opposite of adapting is being *inflexible*. Inflexible people insist on always doing things the same way, even if the situation has changed. This inflexibility is often caused by confusion about what to do.

Instead of being inflexible, look around. Notice how other people are adapting. Then listen. Your friends are probably trying to tell you what you need to do.

You can prioritize

1 Adapting to changes that create risk of harm or injury
  ... comes before...

2 Adapting to changes that can cause big inconveniences
  ... which comes before...

3 Adapting to changes that make minor inconveniences
  ... which comes before...

4 Adapting to changes that don't matter

4. People

> ### Jeremy frowned and craned his neck to see what the holdup was.
> The line had stopped moving. Something was going on.
>
> Then he spotted it. A woman with four young children was butting into the line ahead of him. People seemed to be letting them in. Unbelievable!
>
> "Hey!" he called out. "Get to the back of the line like everybody else!"
>
> The people ahead of him whipped around. "Stop being so rude!"
>
> "Who's being rude?" Jeremy retorted. "They're the ones butting in line!"
>
> His best friend muttered, "Boy, you have a lot to learn about manners."
>
> Jeremy was perplexed. He had no idea what he'd done wrong.

Societies have long-standing patterns about how people should behave with other people. These patterns help us avoid hurting or annoying others.

For this reason, the people around you are an important part of your context. Patterns based on the *age*, *familiarity*, *roles*, and *customs* of the people you are with determine what actions are appropriate and what actions are not.

Everyone has expectations about how others will behave around them. You do too. Following the expectations of others helps everyone feel respected and accepted.

You can prioritize

1. The needs of elderly people
   ... and...
2. The needs of young children
   ... come before...
3. Your needs

Age

How old are the people around you? Are they a lot younger than you? About the same age as you? Much older than you? How old people are affects how you should act near them.

Consideration for weaker people

You are supposed to show care and concern for people who are weaker than you. Age affects a person's strength, health, power, and independence. For example, a toddler has less strength, power, and independence than you, and so does a frail, elderly aunt.

If you are the stronger person, then you have a duty to take care of much younger or much older people. This means treating them with extra respect, kindness, and helpfulness. Let them go before you. Be helpful and considerate—and never show anger or annoyance.

Respect for more powerful people

You are supposed to show respect for people who have earned a high social position, and age often affects a person's social position. A parent has a higher position than a child and is older than the child. Co-workers and siblings have about the same position.

People expect you to show that you acknowledge someone's position. This usually means treating older people with respect and cooperation. Anything that looks like "bossing around" older people is demeaning to their position.

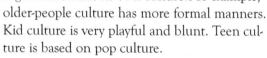

Acceptance of generational culture

You are supposed to accept the culture of different age groups. Each generation has its own culture. For example, older-people culture has more formal manners. Kid culture is very playful and blunt. Teen culture is based on pop culture.

People expect you to show that you respect other age groups. This doesn't mean imitating them, just going along with their ways without criticizing them.

Familiarity

Familiarity means how well you know the people you are with. Are they close friends? Relative that you hardly ever see? Complete strangers? How well you know them is part of your context. People expect you to adapt what you do and say to your familiarity with these people.

When you are with familiar people, you can...

- be informal (e.g., use slang)
- talk about shared experiences (e.g., memories)
- share and exchange (e.g., share food, trade favors)
- trust each other (e.g., you don't need lawyers)
- touch each other (e.g., pat on the back)
- make assumptions (e.g., you know what they like)

When you are with unfamiliar people, you must...

- avoid offering to share
- avoid informal manners and speech
- avoid touching

People assume

... that you are aware how familiar you are with others.
Familiarity affects social patterns and feelings of safety.

People expect

... that you will not use familiar behavior with unfamiliar people.
It makes people feel awkward and uncomfortable.

Rate your familiarity with someone

Familiarity can be high or low. Before you jump in to talk or interact with someone, assess how well you know that person.

Level 1: *close friends and close family members*

Level 2: *friends, neighbors, and relatives*

Level 3: *distant relatives and acquaintances*

Level 4: *people you have just met*

Level 5: *strangers or near-strangers*

Rate Your Familiarity with These People

_____ A same-age person you have just met at a ball game because she sat beside you. You know her name and just a little bit about her.

_____ Your same-age next-door neighbor. You've been friends since early elementary school and have some hobbies in common, so you see each other a lot.

_____ Someone who sat beside you in chemistry at your last school, but you haven't seen each other in a couple of years.

_____ A new co-worker who was hired yesterday. You know his name and position. There is a resume in the files that you can look at too.

_____ The coffee shop clerk who sells you your morning coffee every day.

Once you've assessed how familiar you are with that person, you can decide how familiar to act. The more familiar you are, the more relaxed, casual, and personal you can be.

It's more of a mistake to act a little too familiar than it is to act a little too formally. Unfamiliar people can get freaked out if you're too friendly. Touching, sharing, talking about private matters, and standing too close can make them feel unsafe. They may also wonder if you are perhaps a little bit crazy.

Always watch body language when you're interacting with people you don't know very well. If you're acting in a way that makes them uncomfortable, they'll give body language signals. For example, they may back up, suddenly stop talking, or exchange alarmed glances with a friend. If they do, take a step back yourself and switch to a very neutral and safe conversation.

What to do

1 **Assess your familiarity with the people you are with.**
Rate it 1 to 5.

2 **Decide if touching, sharing, exchanging, etc. are acceptable.**
It's better to err on the side of being too formal.

3 **Watch their body language.**
They will signal their discomfort if you do things wrong.

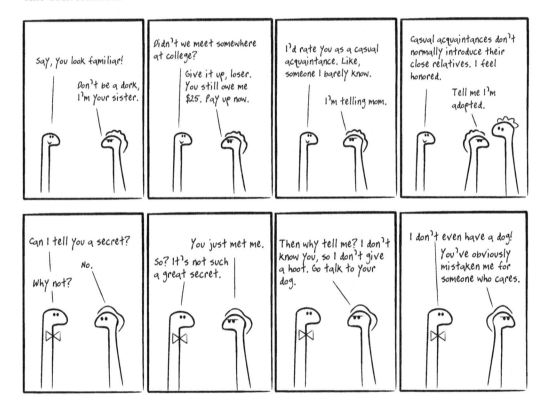

How to introduce people

Introductions are important because talking to a complete stranger feels awkward. Introductions are helpful because they remove this awkwardness.

How to introduce a friend to a friend

- Give the person's name.
- Add one fact that the two people have in common (so that they can start talking right away).
- Repeat for the other person.
- Let them start talking to each other.

> "Louise, this is Jake. He was the best man at Kenny's wedding. Jake, this is Louise. She lives next door to Kenny's sister."

How to introduce yourself to a stranger

- Keep it simple. Watch body language to make sure that the other person doesn't seem alarmed.
- Give your name.
- Add a question about something in the context.

> "Hi, my name is Jake. Are you late for this presentation too?"

- Always introduce yourself when you need to talk to a stranger. It's considered rude to leave someone wondering who you are.

> "Hi, I'm Louise Brown. I'm from the layout department. Mr. Allan told me to come down to get the art files for the new book.

Roles

A role is like a job. Being a student is a role. So is being an employee, a boss, or a best friend. Wherever people have responsibilities to each other, they have roles. Roles are part of your context because they are patterns.

Examples of roles:

- **In a store:** customers, staff, managers, security staff, cashiers
- **At a sports game:** team members, referees, team captains, coaches, offensive and defensive players, goalies, spectators
- **In a college:** roommates, instructors, classmates, club convenors, dorm heads

- **In a family:** parents, children, siblings, spouses, grandparents

How you act depends on your role and on the roles of everyone else around you. In a classroom, the role of the student follows a different pattern than the role of the instructor. Also, what's okay also depends on whether the instructor is in the room or not in the room.

Sometimes the patterns for roles are written down. For example, a school may have a written code of conduct for students and a staff manual for the instructors.

But some roles are informal and don't have written rules. For example, being someone's girlfriend is an informal role.

Also, in a conversation, you might have the role of being the listener. This means your job is just to listen, not to talk—and especially not to change the subject because you're bored. The listener role may last just a few minutes before you get the talker role again.

If understanding roles doesn't come naturally to you, then always ask yourself:

- *What are my responsibilities to everyone in this situation?*
- *What are the roles of the other people?*
- *What do they expect from me?*
- *What actions will make me appear as if I'm trying to take over someone else's role? Will that person be annoyed or relieved?*

People assume

... that you are aware of everyone's role
Because roles affect your relationship with each other.

You can prioritize

1. **The needs of formal roles, such as jobs**
   ... *usually come before*...
2. **The needs of informal roles, such as friendships.**
   But not always. It depends what matters most to you in the long run.

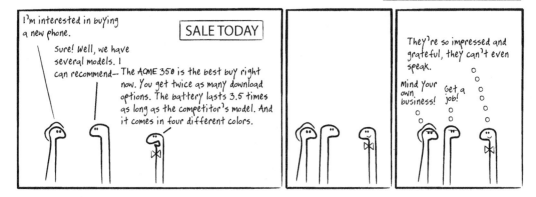

Roles and need-to-know

How much you should tell someone depends on their role. What do they need to know for their role? What do they *not* need to know? Avoid telling someone more than they need (or want) to know.

People like to feel comfortable in their role. Telling them too much makes them feel awkward and embarrassed. Consider need-to-know before you start spilling out details.

Assessing Need-to-know

Role	Need to know	Don't need to know
nurse	name, weight, blood pressure, reason for visiting the doctor	✗ lists of symptoms, details of your personal life, embarrassing information
doctor	detailed symptoms, your questions and concerns	✗ details of your personal life (unless relevant to your health)
counsellor	details of your personal life, worries, plans for the future	✗ tax information, bank account balance, debts
accountant		✗

Need-to-know with friends

How much should you tell to a friend? It depends on your familiarity with that friend. Confiding is a pattern in a friendship. Not all friendships include confiding.

Confiding grows over time. At first you confide simple everyday facts and preferences, like *I forgot my watch.* You might include exchanges, such as *I don't like seafood. Do you?* By offering an exchange of confidences, you allow the friendship to become more confiding.

Never confide more than the friendship is used to unless you ask permission: *Can I talk to you about something kind of personal? I really need some advice.* Also, don't rush to start confiding. The relationship has to grow and develop first. Otherwise you risk alarming your new friend.

Customs

Customs are based on expectations. Every school, workplace, and organization has its own customs and traditions. When you are with those people, you are expected to follow the group's patterns.

Customs take the guesswork out of daily life. They let you know what the right choices are so that you don't have to make hundreds of decisions throughout the day. Once you know the customs, you can fit in.

When you go to a new school or a new job or are in a new situation, observe the customs for a while so that you can learn what people expect.

Blending in vs. being an individual

Everybody wants to be an individual. But people still expect you to blend in with their customs and traditions so that everyone feels comfortable.

Blending in means *watching what others are doing, then trying to do more or less the same thing.* The goal of blending in is to match the patterns that everyone else is using.

Blending in means not standing out. In fact, you try to feel like one of the group, instead of just like yourself. Blending in often means giving up a bit of your individuality so that you fit in.

The effort to blend in may feel annoying. But to others, it is very helpful. Blending in helps people relax. They like knowing that they will not be startled by unexpected and disturbing actions. They also like knowing that their group activities will go smoothly because everyone is cooperating and matching the patterns.

When to blend in:

- *when you are in a new place or with new people*
- *when you aren't sure exactly what normally happens in this place*
- *when the purpose of the place is to relax and have fun*

When not to blend in:

- *when the purpose of the place is to be creative, artistic, or original*
- *when other people are behaving badly*
- *when you are with close friends who are used to you*

Summary

Common sense means being aware of your context. It means making logical predictions and figuring out what people expect based on...

- **the place:** where you are and what people expect you to do (or not do) in this place
- **the time:** choosing good timing
- **the situation:** watching for changes in details that change the purpose of the place
- **the people:** who is nearby, how old they are, how well you know them, what their roles are, and what customs they follow

One you've got a handle on the context, you can start learning common sense strategies for sizing up your situation.

Chapter 2
Perspective

Leila had to make a decision today:
to accept a scholarship from the small but respected arts college in a nearby city, or to accept a position (without scholarship) at the much bigger arts college a day's travel away. Money was tight, so the scholarship was very appealing. But she also liked the prestige of the big-name school.

"I don't know what to do!" she wailed. "What's the right answer?"

"It depends how you look at it," her career counsellor said. "If you look at it just from the perspective of money, the answer is easy. But if you look at it from the perspective of your future, the answer is less clear. You have to look at this decision from different angles to get the full picture. On the one hand, financially, the scholarship is the right choice. But on the other hand, there's more to college than just having the bills paid. Does that help?"

"Yeah," Leila grumbled. "It tells me that I need to find a career counsellor with only one hand!"

What is perspective?

Perspective is an angle or way of looking at things. Whenever we look at something—an object, a person, or a big decision—we first choose a perspective for looking at it.

A perspective is like a lens because it looks at one part of the big picture in one way. It shapes the way we see things.

When you use several different perspectives, you get the whole big picture. Then you are able to make a good decisions.

Perspective is like a LENS.

Perspective means looking at things in different ways. You can look at a chair from the side, above, below, behind, or in front.

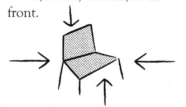

You can also look at it in a mirror, through colored glass, through a magnifying glass, or underwater.

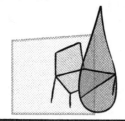

You can look at something from the perspective where you are standing... or upside down from where someone else is standing.

In art, perspective means drawing so that people see the illusion of depth and distance instead of flat paper.

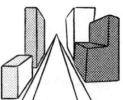

Perspectives allow you to get the big picture.

Perspective

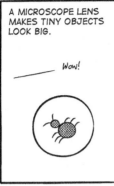

Switching from one perspective to another is like switching lenses. When you look at an optical illusion, you change the perspective you are looking through.

Look at the optical illusion beside this paragraph through the lens of black against a white background. You should see two faces in profile. Now change your lens. Look at the picture through the lens of white against a black background. You should see a fancy vase.

You can also think of perspective lenses like the lenses the optometrist uses to check your eyes. As he/she switches the lenses in the glasses, you see the letter chart differently. Each lens warps your vision in a slightly different way. When the optometrist warps it the right way, you can see clearly.

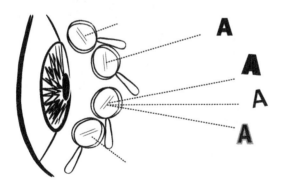

Perspective is also like your eyes. You have two eyes, which are really two perspectives. Each eye sees from a slightly different angle. So when you put them together, you see from two angles at once. That allows you to see in 3D. If you had just one eye, you wouldn't be able to see 3D shapes or estimate distances.

Try this test. Close one eye. Then hold your pencil at arm's length in front of you and lower it slowly so that the point

lands exactly on the far edge of your desk. You probably won't be able to do it. That's because with one eye closed, you have lost your perspective.

Using many perspectives helps prevent over-reacting and under-reacting to situations.

Over-reacting: "Last year, when a bird flew into the classroom window, I got panicky and confused. I wanted to called 911 because I thought it was going to peck us."

Under-reacting: "An old rotting tree behind the track field started falling over. I was standing under it, looking up, not sure if I should move. Fortunately, my friend grabbed me and pulled me out of the way."

1. The context lens

One perspective you can look through is the lens of your context. You examine the things going on around to make sure they make sense in that context. If they don't, you think about the context to figure out why.

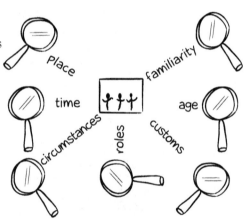

Ask yourself these questions: Does this action or event *belong* in this context? Is it *out of place*? Is there just one or two details that don't make sense in the context? Why?

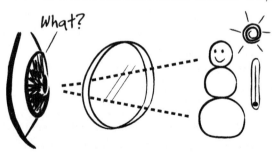

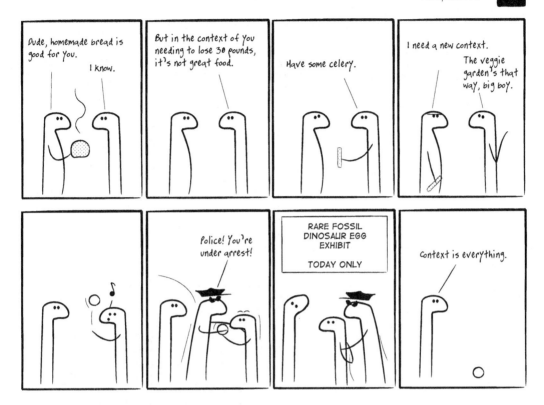

2. The experience lens

Your life experiences are another important perspective. Everything you have learned and experienced in your life is stored in your brain. When you look at a situation, you can see it through the lens of this stored experience. You can compare it to

- **Similar situations from your past:** How is this situation the same as or different from other situations you remember? How did it end last time?

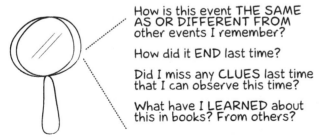

How is this event THE SAME AS OR DIFFERENT FROM other events I remember?

How did it END last time?

Did I miss any CLUES last time that I can observe this time?

What have I LEARNED about this in books? From others?

- **Past mistakes:** What should you do differently this time to avoid the problems from last time?

- **What you have learned:** What did you learn about this topic in school? Is there information in the news, on the internet, or in the owner's manual that could help you understand this situation?

Jill slowed her jogging as she
came near the driveway. Every day this week, at exactly this time, a driver sped out of this driveway without looking. She'd nearly been hit twice.

Jill looked at the situation through her experience lens. She knew that if it happened that way in the past, it was likely to happen again.

She also remembered reading in her driver's manual that many cars have a blind spot in the back corner, where the driver can't see.

She made the decision to cross the street to stay out of harm's way.

3. The strangeness lens

Your strangeness lens compares what's happening to what's normal and focuses on things that don't match. Here are some examples of strange things you might notice:

- a smell that you've never smelled before in this place
- a sound that is much louder than usual
- traffic is that more heavy than usual for this time of day
- weather that is much stronger and wilder than usual
- a familiar dog behaving differently than usual
- someone's behavior that doesn't make sense in the context
- a product that doesn't look or feel like other similar products

What to do

1. **Compare what's happening to the past.**
   Has this ever happened before?

2. **Compare what's happening to what you've learned.**
   Have you read about this?

3. **Use the context lens.**
   Does this make sense in the context?

Rating strangeness

Strangeness can be high or low. Before you decide to take strong action (like running away) or weak action (like ignoring the problem), assess how strange the situation is.

Level 1: Normal: *It matches your memory of what's normal. Nothing is out of the ordinary.*

Level 2: Different: *Something new is happening, but it still makes sense in the context. It is just a different kind of normal.*

People assume

... that you notice when things are strange.
Because strange things stand out against normal patterns.

People expect

... that you will not ignore strange things.
Because they could be dangerous.

You can prioritize

1. **Situations that are alarming**
   ...need to be dealt with before....

2. **Situations that are very strange**
   ...and so on.

Level 3: Strange: *Something new is happening that makes you feel nervous. It doesn't seem normal and doesn't make sense in the context. It makes you look twice and wonder what's going on.*

Level 4: Very strange: *Something new is happening that is very definitely not normal and does not make sense. You don't like it at all.*

Level 5: Alarming: *Something bizarre is happening with a high risk of danger, arrest, injury, or death. You don't know exactly what it is, but you feel you need to get out fast.*

Rate the Strangeness Level (1–5)

_____	A last-minute change to your work schedule
_____	An unfamiliar indicator light flashing on your car dashboard
_____	The sound of a gun firing close by
_____	The sky growing dark in the middle of the day
_____	A dog approaching that is behaving kind of wild and out of control

Strange is not the same as different

Strange is not the same as different. Strange means that something is wrong. Different means something is new, but it still makes sense in the context.

Different...

- *changes one situation into another similar situation*
- *makes sense in the context even though it is new*
- *matches what's normal, even though it feels odd*
- *doesn't create any risk or danger*

There is nothing dangerous or alarming about things that are different. But if you treat things that are different as if they are strange, then you will probably over-react.

Too good to be true

Some strange things seem so good that you can hardly believe it. They seem *strangely* good.

When a situation is **wonderful + strange**, then you should be suspicious.

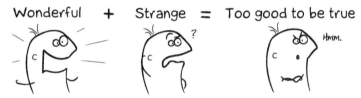

Examples of too good to be true

- You can get something *without work, effort, or money.*
- Someone offers you *a super-sweet deal.*
- Something good happens *unusually fast.*

Just because something seems great doesn't mean you get to drop the strangeness lens. Common sense means knowing when something is too good to be true.

Check Off What's Too Good To Be True

_____ You win a lottery that you didn't even enter.

_____ You get offered a job just five minutes into the interview, even though you thought you weren't qualified.

_____ Your friend tells you that everyone is going to get an B+ in physics as a reward for attendance.

_____ Your boss tells you that you are getting a 10% pay increase this year.

4. The why lens

Asking why forces you to think. It makes you look at the context to decide if an action makes sense. It helps you look at what's happening through your experience lens and rate the strangeness. It also helps you choose the right action.

Examples of why questions:

- *Why is the handle of that frying pan red? Could that mean it's hot? Why would it be hot?*
- *Why is the water shaking in this glass? Is a big truck going by? Is this an earthquake?*
- *Why is the car making that noise? Is it normal, or is it different? Have I ever heard that noise before? Should I stop the car and check it out?*
- *Why does my watch say 10:45 but the wall clock says 12:15? Did one stop working? Which one? Am I late?*
- *Why is everyone looking at me strangely? Am I doing something wrong? Am I in the wrong place?*

What to do

1. **Ask many why questions.**
   They force you to think.

2. **If your questions make you think the situation is strange, rate the strangeness.**
   The stranger it is, the more you need to act.

Perspective

5. The trust lens

Figuring out who to trust is hard. Con artists prey on people who don't have much perspective. They also use people's emotions to trick them into trusting. The trust lens helps you decide who is trustworthy and who is not.

You can probably trust these people:

- a friend of a friend or family member
- a person whose actions aren't strange or unusual

What to do

1. **Avoid trusting people right away.**
   People have to earn trust.

2. **Ask questions to find out their personality.**
   Avoid trusting disrespectful people.

3. **Compare them to people you know.**
   They should be similar to people you already trust.

- a person who treats other people with respect and kindness
- a person who acts like people you already trust
- a person who doesn't act like people you remember who harmed you or others
- a person in a professional helping role

Be cautious about trusting these people:

- a person who is not well known to you or to your friends and family
- a person who acts differently from people you trust

You should probably not trust these people:

- a person who acts in a way that is very strange or too good to be true in the context
- a person who treats other people with disrespect and unkindness
- a person who acts like people who harmed you or others in the past

Would You Trust These People? (Yes, No, Maybe)

- _____ Your mother's best friend for the past 10 years
- _____ Your cousin's girlfriend's brother's classmate, whom you just met
- _____ A new classmate who acts and talks like your regular friends and has a lot of the same interests
- _____ A new classmate with a different accent who is very helpful, polite, and respectful to the instructor
- _____ One of the hotshot students who never pays you any attention who is suddenly talking to you a lot
- _____ A police officer

Trusting experts

A lot of people claim to be experts, but many of them are amateurs, and some are frauds. You can assess how expert they really are by using several perspective lenses.

Context lens: *Is this "expert" part of the community of experts on this subject? Does he/she have the respect of other experts? Does this expert belong with the other experts?*

Experience lens: *Does this "expert" have the kind of education and experience you've seen in other experts?*

Strangeness lens: *Does this "expert" provide background information and evidence for his/her claims? Does the information all make sense? Is anything strange?*

Why lens: *Why is this "expert" interested in this subject? Is anyone paying this "expert" to give certain opinions? Could money be influencing what he/she says?*

6. The priority lens

Another important perspective lens is the priority lens. The priority lens helps you rank different choices based on what matters the most.

Some problems are a "big deal" while others are not. Part of common sense is knowing what's important and what's not. Then you do the most imporant thing first.

> **Level 1: Trivial:** *This is a problem that doesn't really need attention at all. You can't help thinking "Who cares?"*

Level 2: Important: *You really should solve this problem, because it will make a difference to someone. But if you don't get around to it right away, no harm.*

Level 3: Essential: *If this problem doesn't get solved (and soon), then it could cause other bad things to happen.*

Level 4: Critical: *This problem could cause injury or allow other serious situations to happen.*

Level 5: Urgent: *This problem is life-threatening and dangerous and needs attention right now.*

What Problem Is Highest Priority?

_____	You need to drive to a store to buy your friend a birthday card because his birthday is tomorrow.
_____	You need to put gas in the car because it's below empty.
_____	You need to put out a fire in the car engine.
_____	You need to get your sleeping baby sister out of the car seat and out of the car because the engine is on fire.
_____	You need to change the song on the radio because you hate that song.

You can prioritize

1 **Life-threatining situations**
 ...come before...

2 **Harmful situations**
 ...which come before...

3 **Important situations**
 ...which come before...

4 **Trivial matters.**

Short term vs. long term

Prioritizing also mean thinking about what matters in the long term. Something that causes a short problem that goes away quickly is less important than something that causes a long problem that will last for a long time.

Example: Preventing an accident that will break your leg is more important than preventing an accident that will rip your pants. You can sew your pants or buy another pair, but a broken leg will cause you pain and inconvenience for weeks.

You can prioritize

1. **Things that cause long-term problems**
   ... come before...
2. **Things that cause short-term problems.**

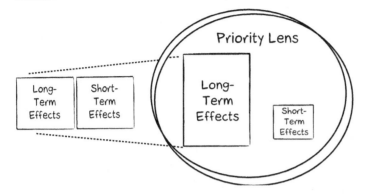

Need vs. want

Prioritizing also means doing the things you *need* to do before doing the things you *want* to do. Make a checklist to help you remember what you need to do.

Example: In the morning, getting ready for the day (eating breakfast, making a lunch, brushing teeth, getting dressed) is more important than playing with your dog, reading a comic book, or listening to music. You can do these other activities if you have time, but only after the necessities are done.

You can prioritize

1. **Things you have to do**
   ... come before...
2. **Things you want to do.**

7. The friend lens

One final perspective is that of your friends. Maybe you aren't very good yet at figuring out what's appropriate in a situation, but very likely some of your friends are.

Whenever you are about to react to a situation, look around and ask yourself:

Are my friends reacting differently than I am?

What about other people I trust?

Am I the only one reacting this way?

When your reactions are different from your friends' reactions—and the reactions of everyone else—you are probably the one who's wrong.

What to do

1. **Observe how others are reacting.**
   Are you reacting differently?

2. **Stop your reaction.**
   Figure out what lenses other people are using that you aren't.

3. **Match your reaction to theirs.**
   Focus on people you trust.

You may looking at the situation through just one lens, without getting the whole picture. Or you may have chosen the wrong action, either over-reacting or under-reacting.

Stop what you're doing. Try to figure out what lenses your friends are using by asking them or observing. Then match your reaction to theirs.

Summary

When you look at situations through just one lens, you see just one part of the picture. It's like seeing with one eye closed—you lose your perspective. Without perspective, you will probably over-react or under-react.

If you look at things from many different angles, using context and experience lenses, then you are more likely to see what's really happening. Use all of these perspective lenses to help you assess your situations accurately and choose the best action:

- **Context lens:** helps you realize what makes sense or doesn't make sense in the context.
- **Experience lens:** helps you compare what you're looking at to your life experience, including your memories, past mistakes, school learning, and reading.
- **Strangeness lens:** helps you decide if what's happening is normal; and if it's not, how strange it is.
- **Why lens:** helps you focus on the reasons behind what you're looking at so that you can decide if action is necessary.
- **Trust lens:** helps you figure out who you should trust or be wary of.
- **Priority lens:** helps you decide what needs your attention first.
- **Friend lens:** helps you realize what's appropriate by comparing your reaction to your friends' reactions.

Once you know how to use perspective, you are ready to learn about a particular type of perspective: the *personal perspective*.

Chapter 3
Personal Perspectives

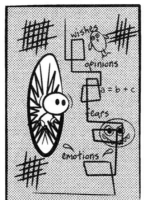

"What?" Leslie cried in exasperation. "I have no idea what you're mad about! All I was doing was helping!"

"You just reached your hand over mine and started typing on my keyboard," Jane said, just as exasperated.

"I was fixing your mistakes."

"I didn't ask you to fix them. I want to do it myself."

"Then why didn't you say so?" Leslie asked.

"Because I shouldn't have to say so," Jane retorted. "You're supposed to know not to take over my keyboard."

"How would I know if you don't tell me?"

"Because the last time you did that I got angry," Jane said. "And I told you it's rude to assume you can correct anybody else's work without asking."

"So, like, do I have to keep records now?" Leslie fumed.

What are personal perspectives?

Your personal perspective is the lens your brain looks through. Everybody has their own personal perspective. It shapes, colors, and interprets everything that person sees and hears.

A person's perspective is full of his/her emotions, experiences, memories, preferences, and beliefs. And it changes depending on what is going on.

Basically, personal perspective is someone's brain and everything in it. People see the world not just through their eyes, but through their thoughts and feelings.

Personal perspectives are like CAMERAS at a movie shoot

A movie shoot usually has at least one camera set far back to give the viewers the wide view for context.

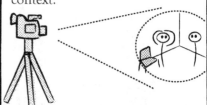

But most of the cameras are positioned over the shoulders of the main characters.

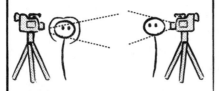

Each camera records what that character sees. This helps the viewers see the action from that character's perspective and understand why the character behaves that way.

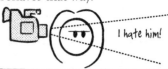

I hate him!

This is why these usually isn't a camera over the shoulder of the bad guys. The director doesn't want the viewers sympathizing with anyone but the good guys.

Bwa ha ha!

Personal perspectives shape what people see and don't see.

1. Wants, needs, and feelings

Imagine everyone wearing different glasses, some with colored lenses, some with warped lenses, others with scientific lenses, and yet others with poetic lenses. This is how personal perspective works. Even when looking at the same thing, we all see it differently.

Psychologists use inkblots to find out what is in someone's personal lens. People look at the inkblot through the lens in their mind. Their answers reveal what's on their mind.

What do you see in the inkblot beside this paragraph? Write it down. Then ask some other people what they see. Compare the answers. Do their answers give any clues about what thoughts are in their head?

What's in your personal lens?

- your ideas about what you want or need
- how you think about and understand things
- how you like to do things
- how you feel
- what you know and don't know
- what you like, dislike, prefer, and want to avoid

People assume

...that you see what they see.
Because to them it's normal.

People expect

...that you try to see things from their point of view.
Because you will be more considerate.

What's in someone else's personal lens?

- that person's ideas about what he/she wants
- that person's ideas about what he/she needs
- how that person thinks about and understands things
- how that person likes to do things
- how that person feels
- what that person knows and doesn't know
- what that person likes, dislikes, prefers, and wants to avoid

You can prioritize

1. **Other people's needs and feelings**
   ...come before...

2. **Your own needs and feelings.**
   That's what being considerate means.

People expect you to see things from their point of view. They assume you've learned to see the world from other people's perspectives. They also believe that you see things pretty much the way they see things.

If you look at things just from your own perspective, then people will assume you are self-centered. They'll assume you don't care what they think or feel. Put other people's needs and feelings before your own to show that you are considerate.

Personal Perspectives

Seeing someone else's perspective

You can't know what's in someone else's personal lens, but you can imagine it fairly accurately. Here are some ideas to help you imagine someone's perspective:

- **Follow the person's gaze:** Look at what he/she is looking at. People usually look at things they are thinking about.

- **Look at facial expressions:** Does the person look happy, content, fearful, annoyed, or angry? People's faces show their feelings. If the person is looking at something with an angry expression, then their thoughts are negative.

- **Consider the context:** Where is the person? What's going on all around him/her? People's thoughts are usually affected by whatever's going on around them.

- **Remember what the person has said:** People often talk about their opinions, likes and dislikes, fears, and pet peeves.

- **Remember how the person has acted in the past:** If you notice that they always react a certain way in the same situation, then imagine what thoughts are making them react that way.

Predicting with personal perspectives

If you've spent a lot of time with someone, you've seen his/her reactions to many different situations. You're now aware of some of his/her wants, needs, and feelings.

What to do

1 **Follow the gaze.**
People look at whatever they are thinking about.

2 **Look at the face.**
People can't help showing their feelings.

3 **Look at the context.**
People's thoughts are based on what's going on around them.

4 **Remember the past.**
People's ideas and opinions don't change very much.

You can predict

1. **Imagine their point of view.**
   What's important to them? Is something nearby?

2. **Remember what you have learned about this person.**
   Relate it to what's happening.

3. **Imagine the person following his/her pespective.**
   Most people make decisions based on their thoughts and feelings.

When you know someone's perspectives, you can predict how he/she will probably react in a situation.

- ■ *If you know he has angry or fearful thoughts about this situation, you can expect him to react angrily or fearfully.*
- ■ *If you know she really wants something, you can expect her to try to get it.*
- ■ *If you know he's relaxed and happy right now, you can expect him to be cooperative.*
- ■ *If you know she has strong opinions about something, you can expect her to take actions based on those opinions.*
- ■ *If he's looking at an object, you can expect him to say or do something related to that object.*

It can be hard to focus on someone else's perspective if you are used to just thinking about your own. But people expect you to see things from their point of view.

When you don't, they take offense. They assume you are being self-centered on purpose.

Remember that other people are always imagining what *you* are thinking about too. They listen to your words, watch your body language, and remember things they've seen or heard in the past to figure out what's in your personal lens.

If you are aware of this, you can control it. Be careful not to let your words, attitude, or actions give away your thoughts, especially thoughts you'd like to hide.

2. Memories and experiences

A person's personal perspective also includes his/her memories and experiences. Everyone's memories and experiences are different.

One person can have a personal lens full of bad memories and experience, while another has a lens full of good memories and experiences.

Those memories can also get mixed up with old feelings. So even though memories and experiences in the personal perspective are very important, they aren't always accurate.

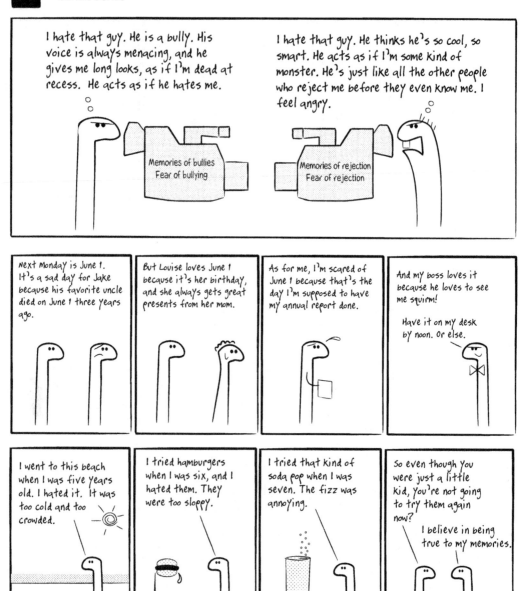

3. Facts and information

People have information in their personal lens that you need... because you don't know everything.

Your personal lens lets you see only a small part of what's really out there. So you need to know what other people see.

What do they know that you don't know? What have they

heard, learned, or read? Add their knowledge to yours by asking questions.

Why ask questions?

- **to get information that you don't have:** *When are we supposed to leave?*
- **to get a second opinion:** *I think the motor sounds strange today. Do you?*
- **to get access to someone else's learning:** *Could you show me how to do this, since you've already read the manual?*
- **to let people know you care what they think:** *We can take the bus. Is that okay with you?*
- **to figure out if someone is trustworthy or not:** *What evidence do you have to support this theory?*
- **to get information that only the person him/herself would know:** *Why are you doing that?*

People assume

... that if you don't ask, then you already know.
Silence sends the message that you have no questions.

How to ask questions

The goal of asking questions is to get information.

- *Listen to the answers.*

- *Ask for feedback to make sure you understand.*
- *Don't assume you already know what the person is going to say.*

GOOD	INSTEAD OF...		

"I know, I know! You don't have to tell me!"

Jeremy pressed down the clutch and tried once again to switch gears. There was a loud, grinding sound.

"Jeremy!" his dad said sharply from the passenger seat. "You're not even listening! I'm trying to explain to you how to–"

"Because I already know!" Jeremy tried to shove the stick-shift again. It wouldn't move. "Stupid thing, it doesn't even work!"

He pounded the steering wheel. The windshield wipers came on. He howled. "Why doesn't this dumb thing work?"

His dad said nothing. Jeremy looked at him.

"When you're ready to listen and learn from someone who actually knows how to drive, then we'll start again," his dad said quietly.

"But I read the manual!"

"A manual can't teach you how to drive."

Jeremy took a slow breath. "Okay. Please tell me what I'm doing wrong."

What to do

1. **Ask questions and listen to the answers.**
   Focus on getting information.

2. **Get feedback.**
   Ask if you got it right.

3. **Don't assume you already know the answer.**
   Otherwise why are you asking?

4. Personal mirrors

Someone's personal perspective also includes a personal mirror. The mirror is how the person sees him/herself. This mirror is full of his/her opinions and ideas about him/herself.

You see yourself in a personal mirror too. Since you see yourself from inside your head, your mirror usually gives you a distorted picture of yourself. Other people see you differently.

Think for a moment about when you look at yourself in a glass mirror. The face you see is actually backward. This is why sometimes you don't recognize yourself in photographs. Photographs show you the way other people see you.

When you sing or talk, you hear your voice from inside your head. If you listen to a recording of your voice, it will sound very different.

So the way you view yourself is usually distorted. The same is true for other people. How they see themselves is usually not accurate.

Picturing someone's mirror

- **Remember things the person has said:** He told me last week that he thought he wasn't smart enough for college.

- **Remember things the person has done:** She always smiles when she volunteers to chair our meetings. I think she thinks she's good at it.

- **Watch body movements and facial expressions:** He always stands at the back of the group during fitness class. He probably thinks he's uncoordinated and doesn't want people to see.

Predicting with personal mirrors

When you know a lot about someone's personal lens and mirror, you can predict their behavior.

- **Consider his/her personal lens:** How does he/she see the world? What are his/her wants, needs, and feelings?

    She always says she believes in magic. I think she'll believe what this fortune-teller tells her.

- **Consider his/her personal mirror:** How does he/she see him/herself?

    If he thinks he isn't smart enough for college, I suspect he'll avoid applying, or he'll come up with excuses.

- **Consider the context:** What's happening? How does it affect the person's lens and mirror?

    His dog has been very sick, and he's worried. I bet he's going to be very irritable today.

You can predict

1. **Think about their personal lens.**
   What are their wants, needs, and feelings?

2. **Think about their mirror.**
   How do they see themselves from inside their head?

3. **Add the context.**
   How does what's going on affect their thoughts?

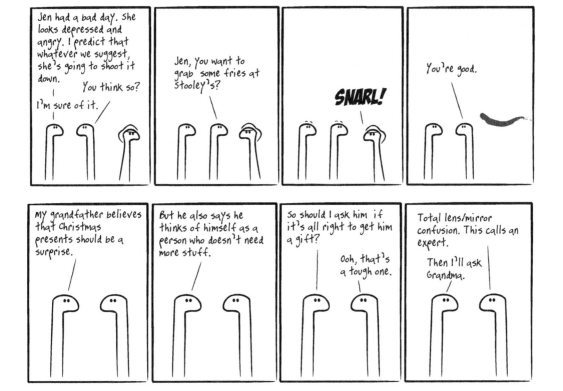

How would these people react if a huge beetle flew in the window?	
Personal lens and mirror	**Probable reaction**
Louise thinks insects are gross and scary. She believes she is not very tough.	Louise will scream and run away.
Isaac thinks science is cool and fascinating. He believes he is a scientific learner.	Isaac will get close to the beetle and observe it.
Penny wonders if aliens in disguise are trying to contact earth. She isn't very sure of herself most of the time.	Penny will look at the beetle without getting too close.
Sam acts quickly without thinking. He sees himself as a get-it-done person.	

5. Different kinds of normal

Normal doesn't exist—it's just an opinion. What's normal in your personal perspective might be very strange in someone else's personal perspective.

Normal is a kind of personal lens. People see things through their ideas of what's normal. If they see something that doesn't match their idea of normal, they believe it's weird.

Predicting with "normal" lenses

You can predict someone's reaction if you know what they think is normal.

If your friend thinks it's normal to handle animals, he won't have a problem playing with your hamster. But if he thinks it's weird to handle animals, he won't want to touch it. If another friend thinks it's normal to drive ten hours to visit relatives, she won't complain about another long trip. But if she is used to living close to her relatives, even a three-hour trip will seem outrageous.

Using the "Normal" Lens to Make Predictions

"Normal" Lens	Probable Reaction
Xian eats a lot of sea vegetables, fish, rice, and stir-fried vegetables. What would he think of a hamburger with ketchup and relish?	He would probably not want to eat it. If he did eat it, he would probably think it tasted weird.
Sarah eats a lot of meat, potatoes, cooked vegetables, and bread. What would she think of a hamburger with ketchup and relish?	She would probably want to eat it. If she did eat it, she would probably think it tasted fine.
Joey has been taking care of his younger brothers and sisters since they were born. How would he react to taking care of a baby?	He would probably not be afraid. He would probably do it very confidently.
Les doesn't have any brothers or sisters and has never done any babysitting. How would he react to taking care of a baby?	

The senses in the "normal" lens

People experience the world through their senses. Everyone's senses are slightly different, so they experience the world differently.

If you have extra-strong senses...

- You may feel things more than other people.
- Bright lights may seem extra-bright to you.
- Spicy food may seem extra-hot.
- Smells might drive you out of the room.

Be aware that other people may not experience these extreme sensations the way you do.

If you have some extra-mild senses...

- You may not feel things as much as other people.
- You may have a hard time reading the blackboard or presentation slides.
- You may put hot sauce on all your food just so you can taste it.
- You may not be able to smell certain kinds of smells.

Be aware that other people may experience these sensations much more strongly.

You can predict

1. **Think about what the other person considers to be normal.**
   Include the senses.

2. **Compare their normal lens to the new situation.**
   Is it what they're used to?

3. **Predict the most likely reaction.**
   People like the things that feel normal to them.

---

6. The need to form conclusions

People are always trying to decide what makes you act the way you do. They want to know whether you are doing things accidentally or on purpose. They form conclusions based on what they see you do and hear you say—and on what they think you are thinking.

People make conclusions about...

- **motives:** *He's behaving that way because he wants to annoy us.*
- **personality:** *Only jerks do that kind of thing.*
- **likes and dislikes:** *He must like red because he wears so many red shirts.*
- **intentions:** *He sounds as if he's about to storm out of the room.*
- **feelings:** *If she stamps her feet like that, then she must be feeling angry.*
- **wishes:** *If she works that hard, then she must really want to earn a lot of money.*
- **thoughts:** *He looks upset, so he must be thinking about yesterday's accident.*

Be aware that actions speak louder than words. If you say one thing but do something that gives the opposite message, people will form their conclusions on your actions, not your words.

Why do people form conclusions?

Most people need to feel that their world makes sense. If the world seemed chaotic and random, they would not feel safe. They form conclusions about people so that their world makes sense to them.

People are like amateur detectives. They use their observations and their common sense to make predictions. But they don't spend enough time at it to get it right all the time. Often their conclusions about you are wrong.

The Human Detective

Once people form conclusions, it's hard work to get them to change those conclusions. So most people try to prevent false conclusions about themselves by always imagining how other people see them.

Watching the movie of you

When people look at you through their personal lens, it's as if they are watching the movie of you. They are trying to figure out what the movie is about.

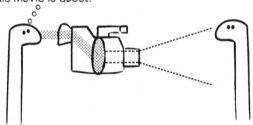

People assume

... that you know they are watching you.
And forming conclusions about you.

People expect

... that you will change your actions if you want them to form different conclusions.
Because that's what they'd do.

Does your action appear deliberate or accidental? Mean or careless? What are you thinking when you act like that?

They compare their movie of you with the movies of other people they know. They also compare it to their movie of themselves. They make conclusions quickly as they go along, because the movie keeps on playing and changing.

What to do

1. **Imagine their perspective.**
   See yourself as they see you, not from inside your head.

2. **Think about what conclusions they could form based on what they see.**
   If you look as if you're being self-centered, they will assume you are self-centered.

3. **Watch for body language.**
   Facial expressions change when people are forming conclusions.

4. **Adapt what you're doing.**
   ...if it looks as if they are forming false conclusions.

How to prevent false conclusions about you

You have some control over the kinds of conclusions people make about you.

- **See yourself from the other person's perspective.** Imagine a camera in the air pointing at you. What would it see as you are talking and acting? That's what other people see. Always think about what conclusions people might form based on what they see you doing.

- **Observe body language and expressions:** When people form conclusions, their facial expression changes. They might raise their eyebrows (if they are shocked or surprised) or frown (if they think you are being self-centered). They might stare at you for a moment as if they are trying to figure you out, or as if they are waiting for you to say something else (such as an apology).

- **Change what you are doing:** If you sense a false conclusion forming, do some other "opposite" action or apologize to undo the false conclusion quickly.

Predicting False Conclusions

What I did	What I look like	Probable conclusion
I repeated an ethnic joke I heard. It was a funny joke.	I look like someone who enjoys making fun of others.	People will conclude that I am racist.
I am never on time for my science lab group meetings. I have a hard time keeping track of time.	I look like someone who doesn't try very hard to be on time.	People will conclude that I am lazy and that I don't care.
I didn't help with the cleaning up after the party. I was thinking about other things and didn't even notice the mess.	I look like someone who wants to come to a party for the fun but not for the work.	_____

Rachel believed she had a great sense of humor. She was always making jokes about her friends. She thought they thought her jokes were funny.

But lately she started noticing that people weren't actually laughing at her jokes. They were just smiling and looking away. Their smiles were tight, unhappy, and very short. Sometimes they frowned. She started thinking that maybe something was wrong.

She considered her jokes from their perspective and wondered if she was hurting their feelings. If she was hurting them, then she knew they'd assume she was doing it on purpose. Maybe her friends were concluding that she was mean and sarcastic.

So she stopped telling jokes about her friends and apologized to them individually, in case any of her jokes had hurt anyone's feelings.

7. Manners and social rules

Nobody knows for sure what's in someone else's personal perspective. We guess, based on what we see, hear, and remember. So how do people accommodate all these different perspectives? What if you don't even know the person? What if there are several people around you, all with different perspectives?

Society has developed a set of shortcuts to help you make quick decisions to accommodate anyone's perspective. They're called *manners and social rules*.

Manners and social rules are patterns of behavior that have stood the test of time. People use them *because they work*. Manners and social rules allow you to do the right thing for other people without thinking and working too hard.

You know how you feel when someone is impolite or inconsiderate around you. What kinds of conclusions do you make about that person? You probably conclude that the person is rude or self-centered—that's how it looks from your perspective.

That is how someone else reacts when you do the same thing. When you forget to use tried-and-true manners and follow social rules, people form conclusions about you.

People assume

... that you choose to use manners and social rules.
If you choose not to use them, you're doing it deliberately.

People expect

... that you will accommodate their perspectives.
Using good manners is the time-tested way.

Social Rules and Personal Perspectives

Social Rules	My Perspective	Their Perspective
Say *Please, Thank you, You're welcome, Excuse me,* etc.	"What a waste of time! Everybody knows you mean it anyway!"	"Your words make me feel respected and appreciated. Now I conclude that you are kind."
Eat with a fork and knife, use a napkin, and chew with your mouth closed.	"I should be able to eat however I want. Eating isn't supposed to be fancy."	"This meal is pleasant because nobody is grossing me out. I feel relaxed and cheerful."
Introduce people to each other when they meet for the first time.	"I feel awkward introducing people. They can just introduce themselves when they feel like it."	"That introduction helped me feel comfortable. I feel respected. Now I conclude that you are considerate of my feelings."
Always ask before borrowing things.	"I know her very well. She won't mind at all if I just take it."	

  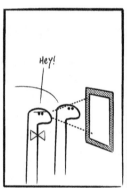 

8. Tact

Tact means considering someone else's perspective before speaking so that you say things that are kind and respectful.

The goal of tact is to avoid hurting or embarrassing someone. So in order to be tactful, you have to know what would hurt or embarrass him/her. The only way to do that is to think about his/her personal perspective.

When you say something tactless because you didn't know someone's perspective, it can be very embarrassing for you, as well as for the other person.

Personal Perspectives

Tactless topics to avoid

Some topics of conversation are tactless because they're about sensitive issues. People feel embarrassed talking about them, or they're afraid of starting an argument.

Avoid asking people questions about (or talking about) these sensitive topics:

- *money and income*
- *personal health issues*
- *sexuality*
- *weight*
- *religious opinions*
- *political opinions*

Tact as a filter

You can think of tact as a filter for words. Filters sift out bad things, leaving the good things in. A tact filter sifts out words or ideas that might hurt or offend someone.

People assume

... that you know how your words and actions affect their feelings.

If you are too blunt, you will be considered cruel and rude.

People expect

... that you will be tactful.

Tact is a form of kindness.

Tact and talking

The tact filter cleans up your words. You use it when you have to say something negative but want to avoid hurting the listener (for example, when turning down a request or giving constructive criticism).

Instead of saying your thought the way you think it, you filter out the hurtful words and replace them with kind words.

Tact and context

Context is an important part of tact. People are always thinking about what's going on around them. To be tactful, you need consider how the listener feels about the context before you speak.

Place: A place can be a tactless context if it makes your message more hurtful. Always choose a place that does not carry memories or associations that will make your message feel worse.

Time: Timing can be tactless if your message interrupts an event where it does not belong. Always choose a time when nothing is happening that could make your message awkward, embarrassing, or extra-painful.

Personal Perspectives

What to do

1. **Imagine their perspective.**
   Think about how they feel in this context.

2. **Choose the context for your message carefully.**
   Avoid situations that might cause the person pain, awkwardness, or embarrassment.

3. **Choose your words carefully.**
   Take the time to find kind words.

Situation: When people are in a situation, they think about that situation. Always imagine their thoughts and feelings about their situation before speaking so that you choose kind words.

People: Tact means thinking about who the person is, not just about your messages. People can become very offended if you show disrespect for their role, age, customs, and familiarity.

Tact and listening

Remember that other people are using tact too. This means that when you are listening, you need to check whether the message has gone through a tact filter. If you don't remove the tact, you will misunderstand the meaning.

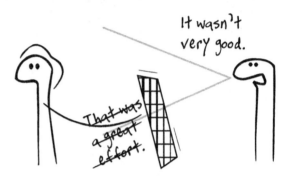

When are people tactful?

- when they have something bad to tell you, and they don't want to hurt your feelings

- when they have something embarrassing to tell you, and they want to avoid broadcasting it
- when they think you are very emotional (e.g., sad or angry), and they don't want to upset you
- when they are trying to avoid sounding as if they are accusing or criticizing

Be aware that when someone has something negative to tell you, that person will try to be tactful. Your job is to filter out the tact so that you understand the message behind the kind words.

How to tell when someone is being tactful:

- **Hesitations:** The person pauses before answering, as if trying to think up how to say it nicely.

- **Indirect answers:** The person doesn't directly answer the question, beats around the bush, or leaves out details. The person is avoiding saying something bad.

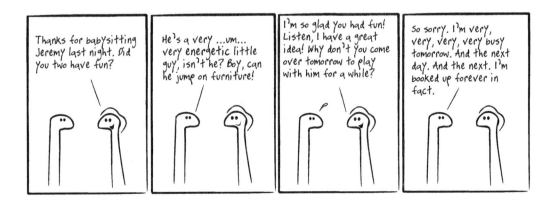

- **We phrases:** The person uses *we* instead of *you* to avoid making their suggestions sound like accusations.

- **Voice clues:** The person's voice doesn't match his/her words. It sounds too sad or serious. Sometimes it just sounds forced, as if the person is acting.

- **Face clues:** The person looks uncomfortable and has a forced smile. This behavior doesn't make sense if the person is complimenting you.

- **Bland words:** The person uses non-enthusiastic words, such as *nice, interesting, maybe,* and *I guess so,* and doesn't go into detail.

What to do

1. **Listen for hesitations.**
   People pause when they try to think up kind words.

2. **Pay attention to the exact words.**
   Weak, vague, and imprecise wording means the person is avoiding stating the truth too bluntly.

3. **Watch body language.**
   A tactful person's body language usually doesn't match his/her words.

Tactful? Yes or No

_____ Your boots stink. Do something about it, will you?

_____ I smell something odd. Do you? Kind of like old socks... or old boots... or something like that.

_____ You did a great job singing up there. I'm proud of you for all the effort you put into this.

_____ Well, to be honest, your singing didn't sound all that great from where I was. Do you have a sore throat?

_____ I'm breaking up with you. You're always negative and boring. I'm tired of it.

_____ I'm so sorry, but I have to break up with you. It's just not working out. It's nobody's fault.

Summary

Figuring out someone's personal perspective requires using your imagination. You have to observe, listen, and remember so that you gradually build up your ideas about how someone thinks. Once you know how that person thinks, you can fairly accurately predict their behavior.

A personal perspective is the camera lens the person uses to see the world. It includes

- **wants, needs, and feelings:** These affect whether the person thinks something is good or bad.

- **memories and experiences:** A person's past affects how he/she reacts to the present.

- **facts and information:** Everyone has different knowledge. Only by asking questions can you learn what they know.

- **a personal mirror:** This is the person's view of him/herself, which is probably not very accurate.

- **ideas about what's normal:** Everybody's normal is different.

As well, you need to remember that people are always trying to imagine *your* personal perspective. They base their ideas on what they see you do and hear you say.

- **People form conclusions:** People are always forming conclusions about you. They do this to make sense of the world and predict your actions. They may end up forming false conclusions about you, especially if you don't look at your actions from their perspective and see what you really look like.

- **People expect you to use social rules:** Good manners are patterns that help you accommodate other people's perspectives. People use them because they work.

- **People use tact and expect you to use it too:** Tact filters outs bad messages so that they aren't hurtful.

Now that you have a handle on context, perspective, and personal perspective, it's time to start applying those ideas to situations where common sense is really handy.

Chapter 4
Safety

Lila buckled her seat belt nervously.

She absently listened to the driving instructor beside her. He might have been saying something important, but there was too much going on in her head to listen.

What if she crashed the car? What if she couldn't even get it started?

"Okay, turn the ignition and then gently drive forward," the instructor said.

Shaking a little, Lila turned the key and gave it a little gas. Sure enough, the car moved.

"Hey, look up," the instructor said. "You're looking at the steering wheel."

"What's wrong with that?" Lila asked. "That's what my hands are holding."

"You need to keep your head up, looking around. That's what will keep you out of accidents."

What is safety?

Safety is a way of seeing. If lots of accidents and mishaps happen to someone, it's not because that person is unlucky. It's because that person doesn't see what's going on.

Safety means being aware of what's around you. It means understanding how everything in the context (place, timing, situation, and people) can affect safety. It also means seeing what's happening around you from many different perspectives.

Only when you really see the safety issues can you respond properly.

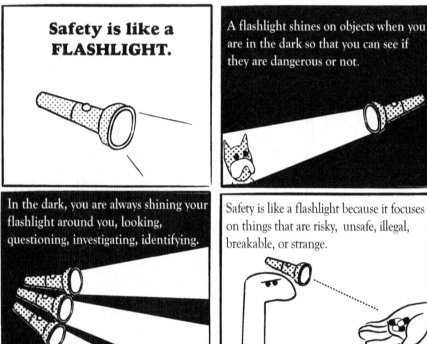

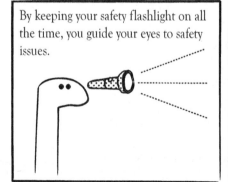

1. Safety as a flashlight

Imagine a safety flashlight in your brain, shining out your eyes. Its job is to guide you around safely and alert you to danger before you walk into it.

Your safety flashlight should be on all the time on the low-beam setting. Low-beams are faint beams that flash around gently as you do other things. They don't take up much of your mental energy, but you should never shut them off.

When your low-beams pick up something strange, they flick to high-beams and look more closely. High-beams are strong beams that focus on things that are out of context or that suddenly appear dangerous. They're also useful when you're in new and unfamiliar situations, when you don't know what's going on or what's safe.

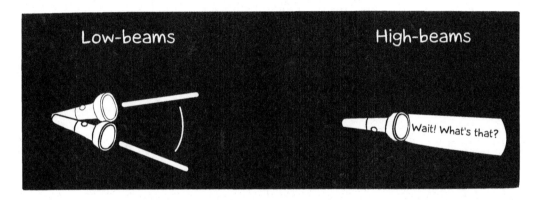

But if your safety flashlight is off all the time, then you won't see these things. You won't notice things that are strange or dangerous in time to react. As a result, you will have a lot of accidents and near-misses... and you will be constantly surprised.

People assume

... that you keep your safety flashlight on all the time. *Keep it on low-beams till you notice something strange or dangerous.*

People expect

... that you will take precautions for their safety all the time. *Otherwise, they'll get angry.*

2. Safety and people

Keeping a safety flashlight on is not just about your own safety. What you do affects the people around you. If you don't see safety issues, then you put other people at risk, not just yourself.

For most people, feeling safe means not being afraid of the actions of people around them. They want you and everyone else nearby to behave in a predictable, reliable way. They expect everyone to look out for their safety.

How people react when your safety flashlight is off

People usually don't tell you if you're acting unsafely. They may just give body language that expresses alarm. But most of the time, they simply leave or avoid being around you without saying anything.

Also, everyone has a different comfort level with safety. That's part of personal perspective. Some people don't like any unsafe activity at all. Other people like a little bit of risk and excitement. Unless you know someone well, assume they prefer always to feel safe.

People expect you to look out for their safety and to prevent accidents. Otherwise, they become angry.

3. Safety and context

People expect

... that you will adapt your actions to your context.

Actions are safe only in certain contexts.

Some actions are safe in some places, times, and situations, but not in others. They's also safe around some people but not around others. You have to adapt your actions to what makes sense in the context.

How can you tell what's okay in a context? By keeping your low-beams on. Scan the context and keep asking yourself if your actions match where you are.

Place:

Time:

Situation:

People:

Carlo couldn't believe his luck.

While cleaning a locked cupboard at the back of the chemistry lab, he found a big glass jar—and it was full of rock candy! He twisted it open and was about to grab a few to pop into his mouth.

Suddenly his friend Jaime appeared at his elbow and grabbed his wrist. "What, are you nuts? Don't eat that!"

"Why not? It's rock candy."

"Rock candy? Is that what the label said?"

"There isn't any label."

"Think about your context, Carlo. You're in a chemistry lab. That's a locked cabinet. Is this likely to be a jar of candy or a jar of something really dangerous?"

Carlo looked at the jar.

"I never thought about it like that."

Accidents and disasters

An *accident waiting to happen* is:

An event + A bad context

= A potential accident

A *recipe for disaster* is:

A combination of events + A bad context

= A potential disaster

Always look around and ask yourself: *What's the worst thing that could happen in this context?* That's the accident or disaster that you want to avoid.

Safety in the 10-second room zoom

When you do your 10-second room zoom, use your safety flashlight at the same time. It's easier to see safety problems before you enter a place than after.

Look for:

- **Odd or unusual behavior:** If your low-beams pick up some odd or unusual behavior, flick on your high-beams and focus on those people. Ask yourself questions. *Are they avoiding a certain area? Are they talking unusually quietly? Is there something they know about that I don't know yet?*

- **Odd or unusual noise level:** If the noise level strikes you as being either too loud or too quiet, flick on your high-beams and watch for body language clues. Ask yourself: *If people are talking extra quietly, then who or what do they want not to hear them? If they are yelling, then why?*

- **Hazards:** Locate any hazards in the room, and remember where they are so that you can avoid them. *Are there objects on the floor that might trip you? Are there dangling objects that could hit your head? Is there anything hot, such as a campfire or stove?*

- **Trouble.** Are any illegal or dangerous activities taking place? Are there any trouble-makers present? Focus your high-beams on them and decide what you should do to avoid trouble. *Is someone vandalizing, street racing, selling drugs, or stealing? Do you have memories of any of these people doing harm to others? If people are goofing around, is it harmless, or is it risky?*

What to do

1. **Flash your safety flashlight for 10 seconds into the room.**
   Take the time to think before entering.

2. **Look for possible problems.**
   Identify the odd, noisy, and risky activities in the room.

3. **Ask yourself questions.**
   Questions force your brain to think.

4. **Enter only after you know the safety issues.**
   You might decide to go home instead.

10-Second Room Zoom

- odd actions
- noise level
- hazards
- trouble

4. Safety and perspective

To be safe, you need to see every situation from many different angles. Seeing only part of the situation is dangerous because you are not getting the "big picture."

The "big picture"

To get the big picture, you need to use many different perspectives. Start with the context and do the 10-second room zoom. Use your perspective lenses, such as the strangeness lens and the friend lens. Compare everything you see to your memories, past experiences, and things you've learned at school or home.

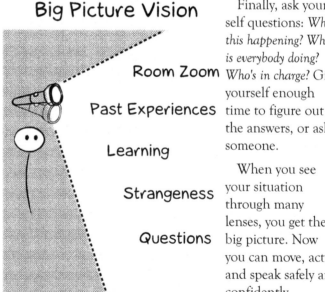

Finally, ask yourself questions: *Why is this happening? What is everybody doing? Who's in charge?* Give yourself enough time to figure out the answers, or ask someone.

When you see your situation through many lenses, you get the big picture. Now you can move, act, and speak safely and confidently.

Safety **107**

Lila liked group driving lessons, because she could sit in the back seat and watch her friend Shelly in the driver's seat.

"Keep your eyes looking way ahead, down the road," the instructor said. "Don't look at the strip of asphalt right in front of your car."

"Why not?" Lila asked.

"Because you want to be looking at where you're going to be in a few seconds," he answered. "And keep glancing to the sides of the road. You want to make sure you see everything."

Lila watched Shelly's eyes dart to the sides, then back to the road in front of her. As the car drove up beside a boy on a bicycle, Shelly saw him in time to slow down and give him extra room.

What to do

1. **Keep your safety flashlight on all the time.**
   Make sure you are getting the big picture.

2. **Zoom the room.**
   Make sure the context is safe and makes sense to you.

3. **Use your experience lens.**
   Compare your situation to your memories and to things you've learned.

4. **Ask yourself questions.**
   If you can't figure out the answer, then ask someone.

The opposite of big picture vision is *microscope vision*. In microscrope vision, your safety flashlight is off because you're focused on your interests or activities. You look only at the small picture. You ignore your context and never think to zoom the room before entering.

Microscope Vision

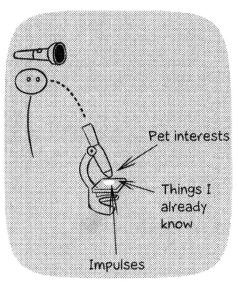

People with microscope vision live "inside their head." They don't pay attention to what's going on around them. The only learning and experience they think about are things related to their favorite interests.

Basically, they're in the dark. And their safety and the safety of people around them are at risk.

You can predict

1. **Scan the room to get the big picture.**
   The more lenses you use, the better.

2. **Identify problem areas.**
   What seems strange, unusual, unreliable, or unsafe?

3. **Predict what might happen with those problems.**
   Do something to avoid them.

5. Safety and personal perspectives

Figuring out what other people are thinking is useful for safety. The best way to do that is to look at their eyes.

Scan your low-beams on the eyes of the people around you. Do it often. Make sure everyone looks calm. If someone looks alarmed, angry, or upset, then focus your high-beams on their face. They may try to signal their anger, worry, or distress to you, or they may send you a silent message.

Scan People's Eyes Frequently

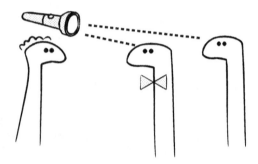

Think of your safety flashlight as a message-sender as well as a message-receiver. Catching someone's eye sends the message that you are aware of him/her. This makes them feel secure and safe.

Flashlight to flashlight, come in, please!

Locking eyes on the road

Catching someone's eye is very important on roads. Drivers, cyclists, and pedestrians all use safety flashlights to scan each other's eyes. That's why drivers expect pedestrians to look up as they approach the road.

When you can see drivers' eyes, you know what they are looking at. This gives you a good idea what they're about to do. If the driver can see your eyes, he/she can figure out what you're about to do.

Safety | 109

Lock Eyes with Drivers

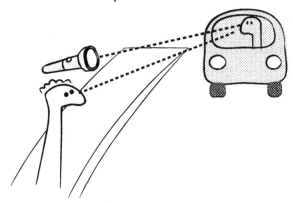

Locking eyes on the road helps you figure out what someone can see (and can't see) and what they're looking at (and not looking at).

Locking eyes also sends someone the message that you are aware. If you walk up to a busy street without locking eyes with the drivers, then the drivers may panic. They will not be sure that you can see them, and they may suddenly swerve to avoid you.

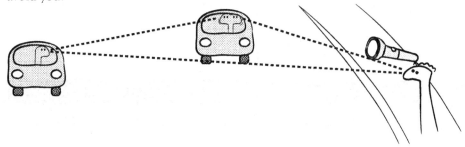

Shen was walking home, worrying about the final report she'd just handed in. Did she do it right? Would the instructor like her research?

As she approached the road, a car suddenly screeched and swerved away from her. Shen's heart thumped in surprise.

"I wasn't going to cross without looking!" she grumbled to herself. "That driver's an idiot!"

Then she realized she'd walked up to the edge of the road with her head down. She hadn't looked around or locked eyes with the drivers. So that driver probably thougth she was about to walk right in front of his car!

Shen carried on, still deep in thought. But when she approached the next road, she lifted her head up and looked around.

You can predict

1. **Lock eyes with drivers.**
   Never approach a road with your head down or looking away.

2. **identify what the drivers are looking at.**
   If they aren't looking at something (or at you), then assume they don't see it (or you).

3. **Follow their gaze to predict what they are about to do.**
   People look in the direction they are about to move.

People expect

... that you will look up as you approach a road.
They want to see your eyes.

People expect

... that you will look at your actions from their point of view.

It's the law.

Personal perspective and crime

People see your actions from their own personal perspective. If your words and actions make them feel afraid, then they consider your actions harmful. Words and actions that cause fear are considered crimes. It doesn't matter what you meant. What matters is how the other person experiences it.

If your words or actions appear to threaten others, or if they seem strangely dangerous to them, then by law, those people can treat it as a crime.

It may seem unfair that the law holds you accountable for how other people see things. But the law expects you to look at your actions from everyone's point of view.

Perspective and Crime

Action	My Perspective	Their Perspective
Grabbing a butter knife and saying, "I'm going to kill you!"	"It's a joke. Nobody's going to take it seriously."	"This is a death threat. You are nuts. I need to call the police."
Repeatedly asking someone out on a date.	"I want her to know how much I like her."	"This is sexual harassment. It's annoying and scary. He won't leave me alone."
Pretending to be a police officer.	"Everyone will think it's funny."	"This is a crime. If people did this, we would not know who the police are."
Hitting someone with a book as a joke.	"Nothing important, just getting his attention."	_____ _____ _____

Personal perspective and personal space

Because people want to stay safe, they have an invisible *health and safety zone* around themselves, like a big bubble. They don't want anything that might bother them to come into that space.

People expect

... that you will respect their health and safety zone.
They want to feel safe around you.

How can you know what would bother someone? Probably the same things that would bother you.

What stays out of someone's health and safety zone:

- **Germs:** Nobody wants to catch someone else's viruses, so keep your coughing and sneezing away.
- **Smells:** Nobody wants to smell your smells, so keep your perfume and body odor away from their sense of smell.
- **Sounds:** Nobody wants to listen to your unpleasant body sounds, so keep your snorting and spitting sounds out of their hearing.
- **Sights:** Nobody wants to see you being unhygienic, so pick your teeth and clean your nose in private.
- **Touch:** Nobody wants you to touch them without permission, so keep your hands away.

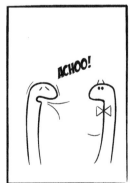   

6. Safety and personal mirrors

Remember how you learned that your personal mirror is the way you see yourself from inside your head? Other people see you very differently—and they're more likely to be accurate than you are.

It's not hard to see how this could become a safety problem. To be safe, you have to be realistic about what you are, what you know, and what you still need to learn. But your mirror can make you think you are smarter, stronger, more expert, and more safety conscious than you really are.

Safety problems occur when there is a big gap between what your mirror says and what's real. You end up doing things that you aren't qualified to do. You try things that you aren't strong enough to try. You take risks because you didn't know that they were risky for you.

If you get in a lot of accidents or near-misses, then it may be the results of distortions in your personal mirror.

Common sense means being aware that your mirror is distorted, but it also means being aware that other people have distorted mirrors too. Other people make bad judgments and hasty decisions too. Just because someone says he/she can do it, that doesn't mean he/she can.

Being aware of possible problems with someone's mirror will help you avoid the safety problems they cause.

Rate your knowledge and skill

You can improve your personal mirror by becoming more aware of your knowledge and skill level. Listen to others when they assess your ability. Remember that they see you more accurately than you see yourself.

Rate yourself:

- **Level 1: Beginner:** *I have no real training yet. I don't really know how to do this (even if it looks easy).*

- **Level 2: Amateur:** *I've worked on this skill for a while and have read the manual. But people tell me I still need more practice.*

- **Level 3: Intermediate:** *I've had some training and practice. I now know the basics. I may feel as if I know everything, but people tell me there is a lot that I don't know yet.*

- **Level 4: Advanced:** *I've learned, practiced, and had instruction. People tell me I have very good knowledge and skills. I feel confident.*

- **Level 5: Expert:** *I've completed all the formal training and had a lot of experience. My qualifications state that I'm skilled enough and qualified enough to teach this skill to others.*

People assume

... that you know what you can and can't do.
Their safety depends on it.

Rate the Knowledge/Skill Level (1–5)

_____ Farmer: I grew up on a farm helping mom and dad every day with the farm chores.

_____ Singer: I'm considered by many people to be the best karaoke singer in town.

_____ Driver: I read the manual and practiced two months with my parents.

_____ Skiier: I trained at a ski school and got all but one of the certificates for every level.

_____ Swimmer: I received lifeguard certification, two certification upgrades, and have a job as a lifeguard.

_____ Rock climber: I've climbed in a climbing gym a couple of times but would like to tackle a mountain. After all, how hard can it be?

Moe watched the waves crashing
over the shore. He couldn't wait to get out there.

"How good a swimmer are you?" the surfing instructor asked. "This beach is only for expert swimmers."

"Me? I'm great," Moe answered, trying to look modest. "I'm a really strong swimmer."

"There's a strong current in these waters," the instructor added solemnly. "I have to know exactly what swimming instruction you've had."

Moe paused and thought for a moment. "I've had some lessons. I guess I'm about an intermediate swimmer. People tell me I need to work on my strokes more."

"Then it's a good thing we didn't head out into these waves," the instructor said, "or you would have been in over your head!"

7. Safety and impulsivity

Impulsivity means acting without thinking first. An impulse can be...

- **A feeling, such as a want or a need.**
  Example: *wanting to be first in line*

- **Acting on a feeling without thinking first.** Example: *shoving people out of the way to be first in line*

There are many causes of impulsivity. One big one is that the thinking part of your brain can be half-asleep. When it's half-asleep, your safety flashlight is off, and your feelings and impulses take over.

Leaving room in your brain for safety

Your brain is like a battery. It can power only so much activity at a time. If you power one activity, you have to turn off the power for another one.

Some people turn off their safety flashlight to concentrate brain power on their activities. But this is a safety hazard. Your safety flashlight needs to stay on all the time. If it's on low-beams, it won't take up too much brainpower.

Be aware that intense activities can turn off the safety flashlight without your being aware of it. This is why in most places it is against the law to use a cell phone while driving.

What to do

1. **Keep your safety flashlight on all the time.**
   No matter what you are doing.

2. **Turn off activities that take up all your brain energy.**
   Always leave some power for the safety flashlight.

8. Safety and fear

Fear is an emotion, not a thought. But it's a very strong feeling that can take over your ability to think.

Some people think they are safe when they are afraid. But being afraid doesn't protect you from harm. In fact, if you panic, then fear can make things worse.

Safety depends on thinking, not feeling. Fear gets in the way of thinking.

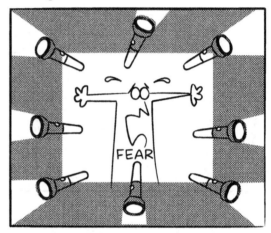

When you are afraid:

- You flash your high-beams wildly, without focusing just on what is dangerous.

- You don't assess your risks, so you can't tell which ones you need to avoid.

- You don't observe whether other people are scared or calm, so you can't get information from them.

- You can't remember how you handled these situations in the past, so you make the same mistakes.

Dealing with fear

The hard part about fear is that it gets control of you very quickly. But there are some ways to prevent and control fear so that you can think clearly.

- **Keep low-beams on to prevent surprises.** Surprises go hand-in-hand with fear. If you get a bad surprise (for example, you step off the curb, and suddenly a car squeals to a stop in front of you), you will react with fear and alarm. But if your safety flashlight is on low-beams all the time, then you shouldn't get these kinds of surprises.

- **Get help with anxiety.** Anxiety is a trickle of fear inside you all the time. This anxiety makes you react more fearfully when things happen than you would if you didn't have anxiety. If you have anxiety, you can get rid of it by getting treatment from a professional. Treatments like neurofeedback, counselling, yoga, meditation, and medications are all very effective.

- **Take a step back and breathe.** When you are scared, you stop breathing normally. Forcing yourself to breathe slowly helps calm you down so that you can think.

- **Identify your fears.** What are you feeling afraid of? Is it something you should be scared of, such as charging animals, gun violence, or falling rocks? Or is it something that's not dangerous at all, such as a sudden change in routine or a dog barking far away? If your fears don't make sense, then tell that to your brain.

What to do

1. **Keep your low-beams on all the time.**
   Know what the dangers are so that you don't get surprised.

2. **Get rid of anxiety.**
   Anxiety makes you feel scared of everything.

3. **Breathe.**
   Slow, regular breathing gets rid of panic feelings.

4. **identify your fear.**
   Make sure you aren't feeling afraid of something non-dangerous.

5. **Be aware if your brain locks.**
   Unlock it by talking to yourself.

Keeping your brain unlocked

Fear can also happen if your brain suddenly locks up and you can't think. You realize that you're not in control. Part of the fear is from awareness that your brain isn't working.

Sudden emotions, shocks, surprises, and not knowing right away what to do can all lock your brain for a moment or two.

When this happens, tell yourself, "I can't think right now." Talking to yourself helps make you aware that your brain is locked, which is the first step toward unlocking it.

In fact, saying anything out loud will help unlock your brain.

Fear, anxiety, and panic all get in the way of using common sense. You have the mental skills to tackle almost any siutation effectively, as long as you keep your brain working. Keeping emotions like fear under control will make you better at thinking your way through a crisis.

Summary

Safety is a way of seeing. It's a type of awareness. Common sense means knowing how to be safe:

- **Use your safety flashlight:** Keep it on low-beams all the time. When you spot something strange, flick it to high-beams to check out the situation.

- **Consider other people:** Everyone expects you to care for their safety as well as your own. Be aware that they don't want unsafe and out-of-control actions going on around them.

- **Think about the context:** Some actions are safe in one context but not in another. Think about the context before you do something. Include your safety flashlight in your 10-second room zoom.

- **Look at the situation through many lenses:** Seeing the situation from different angles gives you the big picture. Don't miss small details that can cause big problems.

- **Consider other personal perspectives:** Look at people's eyes to see what they're thinking and what they're about to do. Avoid doing things that scare people, because those actions are considered crimes. Respect people's personal health and safety zone by keeping your germs, smells, sounds, etc., away.

- **Watch out for distorted mirrors:** Take the time to rate your skill and knowledge so that you're aware of your true ability level.

- **Get control of impulsivity:** Impulsivity is a feeling that can take over your brain. Get professional help with impulsivity before it causes harm.

- **Get control of fear:** Fear is an emotion, not a thought. Like impulsivity, it can get control of your brain. Learn strategies for controlling and managing fear.

Safety is a fairly straightforward area where you can apply common sense. But did you know that common sense applies to relationships just as well?

120   Comic Sense

Chapter 5
Relationships

Kim waited as four, five, six rings

of the cell phone went by unanswered. Her best friend Rona wasn't answering her phone. That was strange. After all, Rona had call display.

Kim clicked off, then punched in the number again.

"What do you want?" Rona answered tersely.

"Oh, hi, Rona. It's Kim."

"I know. I can tell by the number."

"Long time no see."

"Very long. Like, at least eight months."

"I guess so. Well, are you going to Ann's party next week?"

There was a pause. "What's it to you?"

Kim frowned. "Well, I thought we could go together."

"Sorry, I'm going with someone else." The phone clicked off, leaving Kim wondering what was going on.

What is a relationship?

A relationship is a connection with another person. For example, you can have family relationships, friend relationships, romantic relationships, school relationships, and workplace relationships.

Having a relationship is different from owning an object. If you own an object, you can put it away for a year, then dust it off and use it. But if you ignore a relationship for a year, it won't be there when you go looking for it. The relationship will have become empty, and the other person would have given up.

A relationship is like a BANK ACCOUNT. 	The bank account contains all the goodwill (good times, warm feelings, and sense of connection) that you have with another person. 
You can make deposits to this account through words and acts of appreciation, kindness, acceptance, generosity, and good times together. 	But you can also make withdrawals to this account through acts of deception, unreliability, meanness, disrespect, and neglect. 
When your bank account with another person gets too low, the relationship ends. 	**Maintaining a relationship is the same as maintaining a bank account.**

1. Deposits in a relationship

Relationships are like bank accounts because they need regular *deposits*. Deposits are everything *good* that you contribute to the relationship, including just time spent with that person. Deposits add to the goodwill in the relationship.

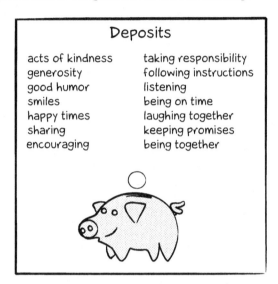

Some people think others don't mind when they get lazy about their relationships, such as when they're late, forget birthdays, ignore promises, or break belongings. But people do mind. Over time, they run out of patience.

That's because acts of neglect and unkindness are *withdrawals* from the relationship. They subtract the amount of goodwill in the relationship.

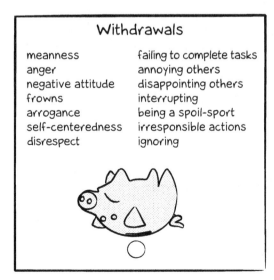

People expect

... that you will make regular deposits to your relationships.
They know that the relationship will dry up without goodwill.

People assume

... that you want a strong relationship with them.
They don't understand why anyone would treat a relationship like a belonging.

Your relationship account with someone goes up and down, depending on how well you take care of it. If it goes down too much, you need to make a lot of deposits to bring it back up. If you don't, then the other person will decide to close your relationship account with him/her.

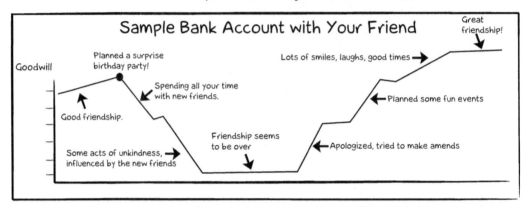

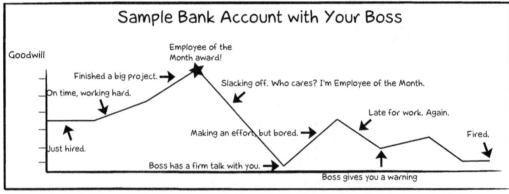

Bank account interest

If you keep a high balance in your relationship bank account, it will grow on its own. The person will start to think positive thoughts about you all the time, even when you are not there. This adds to the goodwill in the relationship.

Relationships

You can predict

1. **Think about how many deposits you make to your relationship bank account.**
   Deposits are good times, cheerfulness, helpfulness.

2. **Think about how many withdrawals you make.**
   Withdrawals are anger, bad times, and neglect.

3. **Subtract.**
   If the balance is negative, the person thinks negative thoughts about you. If positive, the person thinks positive thoughts about you.

But the same is true for a low balance. If your relationship bank account is low, the other person will start to think negative thoughts about you, even when you are not there. This drains your balance very quickly. If you do not fix a low balance, it will erode the relationship without your even knowing.

Costs and benefits

Another way to look at relationship bank accounts is to consider the costs and benefits of a relationship. A cost is something a person doesn't like or that makes things worse. A benefit is something that a person does like or that makes things better.

People get rid of relationships that have too many costs and not enough benefits. Nobody wants to keep a relationship that makes their life worse, not better. People keep relationships that have lots of benefits and few costs.

If you want to keep a relationship, you need to make sure you keep your costs low and your benefits high to the other person.

A high-cost, low-benefit friend

"Jessie is my friend, but I'm tired of her. I always have to fix her problems, respond to her complaining, and do the work when she lets me down. She's always negative and doesn't follow through on her promises. She's self-centered and interrupts a lot. My friends avoid me when I'm with her.

"Jessie's friendship costs too much. I can't afford to keep this relationship."

A high-benefit, low-cost friend

"Seth always helps me with my problems, mostly by listening when I need a listener. He cheers me up when I'm down, and we have a lot of fun together. He's also very dependable and does his share of the work. He's polite, interesting, and cheerful when we're with other people. My friends like being with me when I'm with him.

"Seth provides me with a lot of benefits. I want to keep my relationship with him."

Game relationships

When people play board games or sports games, they play two parallel games at the same time.

One is the *play game*, with its moves and points, and the other is the *relationship game*, with its costs and benefits.

The relationship game is the important one to win. Your goal is to make deposits of goodwill to your relationship accounts with all the other players while playing the play game, so that you come out with a higher account balance than when you started.

Examples of deposits in a game relationship:

- good times, jokes, and laughter
- passing, sharing, and encouraging
- being a good sport, even when losing
- enthusiasm and respect

People assume

... that you play a game to play with them.
You don't play just to win.

People expect

... that you will maintain relationships during the game.
Being a good sport maintains your relationships.

Cost or Benefit?

_____ Lee always does his share of the chores in the house, following the list that he and his roommates set up months ago.

_____ Paul gets angry with his teammates when they start losing the soccer game, because nobody is playing well.

_____ Saul was so busy last week that he didn't have time to get (or make) a birthday gift for his girlfriend.

_____ Shana never argues or complains with her boyfriend Carl, but she argues and complains with all his friends.

_____ Tran listens whenever his brother describes the problems he's having at his new job.

_____ Ella's friend is absent today, so Ella takes notes for her and gets extra copies of the assignments.

Why people like you

People like you based on how you make them feel.

Sure, they *get together* with you because of common interests. But they *stay together* and become friends because of *feelings*. When people make you feel good, you want be around them.

This means that people don't end up liking you because of your clothes, IQ, or hobbies. You don't have to be a perfect person to have good friends. People will like you because they like the good feelings that they get from the relationship with you.

But keep in mind that they will also *dislike* you if they get bad feelings from being around you.

This is true for all relationships:

- **Friends** keep friends who make them feel happy and supported. They don't necessarily keep the smartest, strongest, or coolest friends.

- **Bosses** hire employees who make them feel secure and worry-free. They don't necessarily hire the employees with the highest qualifications.

- **Workers** like co-workers who are dependable, friendly, and cheerful. They don't necessarily like the best workers.

- **Teachers** like students who smile a lot and make them feel calm and confident as a teacher. They don't necessarily like the smartest students.

What to do

1. **Keep your relationship bank account high.**
   High benefits create good feelings.

2. **Provide more benefits than costs.**
   Costs create anger and disappointment.

3. **Focus on their feelings.**
   People like people who make them feel good.

YES	NO
This candidate makes me feel comfortable and relaxed. She makes my worries about hiring a new person disappear. I will hire her. 	This candidate has good qualifications, but he makes me feel uneasy and uncomfortable. His answers make me worried because he doesn't seem to care. I don't feel safe hiring him. 
This date was great because he made me feel important. He listened to me. He made me feel respected because he didn't boss me around. He also made me laugh. I'll go on another date with him. 	This date was very good-looking, but he made me feel nervous and uncomfortable. I felt angry because he was always interrupting me. His table manners made me feel sick. I won't go out with him again. 
This new classmate makes an effort to talk about things I'm interested in. She smiles a lot, and she listens. I'm going to spend more time with her. 	This new classmate never smiles at me. She only gives commands, as if she expects me to obey her. She acts as if she thinks I'm boring. I'm going to avoid being around her. 

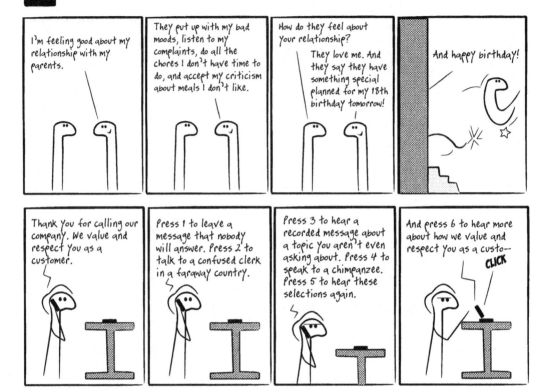

Predicting reactions

Knowing how the relationship bank account works, with its deposits, withdrawals, benefits, and costs, should help take some of the mystery out of relationships.

You can use math to predict where a relationship is heading. All you have to do is add up your benefits and subtract your costs to the other person.

But to that well, you have to be able to think about the relationship from the *other person's perspective*. If you think about it just from your own perspective, you won't consider the costs and benefits *to him/her*. You'll just consider the costs and benefits to yourself.

If you think too much about how the relationship makes *you* feel, then you'll forget that you're supposed to be focusing on how the other person feels.

Does that mean you ignore yourself in a relationship? Not at all—because remember that the *other person* is thinking about *your* feelings and trying to create benefits for you. For the relationship to work, both people have to be making deposits to the other person's account.

You can predict

1. **Consider the deposits and benefits you give to the relationship.**
   Focus on the other person's feelings.

2. **Think about the costs and withdrawals.**
   These drain down your balance.

3. **Subtract #2 from #1.**
   What's left is the balance in your relationship account.

4. **A low balance means the relationship will end soon.**
   A high balance means the relationship is doing fine.

Predicting Reactions

What you do	How he/she feels	His/her thoughts
"I'm in a bad mood, so I yell at my sister and make her walk the dog."	She feels angry, taken advantage of, and abused.	"I wish she weren't my sister! I'm going to stay away from her and never do anything for her."
"The new student forgot his lunch. I had an extra sandwich, so I gave it to him."	He feels grateful and a little bit less lonely.	"This person is really nice. I'm going to return the favor someday."
"The boss wants me to do all this extra paperwork, but I don't want to bother."	He feels disappointed, irritated, and worried about the work that needs to be done.	"This employee doesn't seem to want to help out any more than he has to. If I have to cut staff this year, I'm going to let him go."
"I asked my mom to drive me to the party, then I yelled at her in front of my friends."		

Amy closed the door of her office

and leaned back against it, her heart pounding. Mr. Duke, her boss, had just yelled at her... and for no apparent reason.

Amy felt annoyed and abused, but also a little confused. Was there something she'd done? She thought about the past couple of weeks. Had she created a lot of costs and made too many withdrawals from her work-relationship account?

She'd been late several times. She'd also been really preoccupied with nonwork problems. Several times Mr. Duke had told her to get her reports done, but she could never keep straight which ones were near the deadline. She considered Mr. Duke's feelings. Obviously he was angry. But maybe he was worried too—that the company was going to miss deadlines.

It was easy to see how all this was going to get her fired very soon.

Ten minutes later, she knocked on Mr. Duke's door. He opened, saw her, and sighed. "What is it now?"

Amy swallowed. "I want to apologize. I realize I've been slack on the job this week, thinking about other things. I owe you some extra time, and I'll do it this week."

> She spent the next week working 14-hour days, carefully getting everything done and on Mr. Duke's desk by morning each day.
>
> Mr. Duke stopped her in the hall the next week. "Thanks for meeting all those deadlines. Your reports were very thorough."
>
> He gave a small smile and a nod before he walked on.
>
> Amy felt a wave of relief. She was back in the boss's good books again, and this time, she planned on staying there.

2. Wants, needs, and expectations

People want, need, and expect certain things from a relationship with you. What exactly are those things?

To make people feel good, you have to know what they like. Everybody has different personal perspective, which means everyone has different likes and dislikes.

Just because you like something, that doesn't mean someone else will too. And just because you don't need something, that doesn't mean someone else doesn't need it.

By giving the other person what he/she wants, needs, and expects, you deposit goodwill in the relationship.

What to do

1. **Observe other people.**
   What they like or dislike shows in their face and reactions.

2. **Listen.**
   People talk about their likes and dislikes.

3. **Remember how they reacted in the past.**
   That's a good indication how they'll react now.

4. **Learn the expectations.**
   They don't change much from one place to another or from one person to another.

How can you figure out what the other person wants, needs, or expects?

- **Observe:** Watch the person interacting with others. Look for clues in the person's face and actions about what he/she likes and expects.

- **Listen:** People often tell you what they want, need, and expect from you, especially in formal relationships (like a boss-employee relationship). Friends often use teasing or mild criticism to try to tell you how they need you to behave in the relationship.

- **Remember:** Keep in mind what worked and didn't work in your past relationships. For school and work relationships, expectations are very similar from one place to another.

- **Read:** School and workplace relationships often come with a code of conduct, a contract, or a manual. Read it so that you know how to be a benefit.

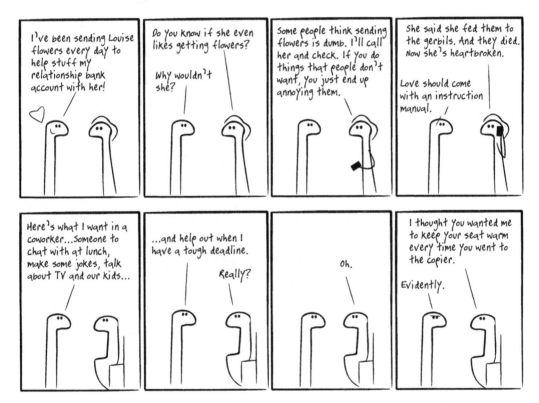

Occasionally people want things from a relationship that you don't want to (or can't) give: for example, *obedience, adoration, excitement, status, money, protection, favors*. They may want you to conform or pretend to be someone that you aren't.

If the other person wants something that you don't think you should give, then don't give it. The costs of that relationship are too high for you. Find someone else to be your friend.

What to do

1. **Be patient.**
   Close relationships grow very slowly.

2. **Spend time together.**
   Only through time together can you learn about each other.

3. **Provide benefits.**
   Build up the goodwill in the relationship as it grows.

3. Close friendships

Friendships develop slowly over long periods of time. It takes a big investment of time to turn an acquaintance into a friend, and even more time to turn a friend into a close friend. Common sense means not expecting a close friendship to develop overnight.

Some people are in a rush to have a close friendship. But you can't go out and "get" a close friendship. Remember: a relationship is not a thing—it's a connection. You have to grow that connection over time.

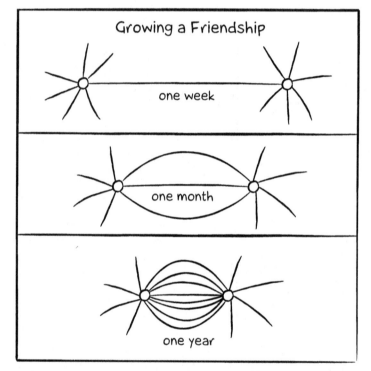

A person starts out as an acquaintance. You meet, get to know a little about each other, and start spending some time together. During this time, you find ways to provide little benefits to that person.

After you spend time learning about his/her personal perspective, he/she becomes a friend.

Later, once you know so much about each other's personal perspectives that you feel comfortable confiding in that person, you become close friends.

Close friends have a lot of history together. This history is full of shared experiences and memories, which help hold the friendship together.

People assume

... that you will wait till the friendship develops.
Enjoy the process of learning about someone.

People expect

... that you won't rush friendship.
That kind of trust takes time to build.

Shared perspectives

To have a close friendship with someone, you need to find out what you have in common. Not just common interests, these can be common feelings, priorities, likes, ideas, and experiences—basically, anything that is part of your friend's personal perspective.

Your friendship grows when you and your friend learn about each other's perspective, discovering where you have a *shared* perspective. This shared perspective is like the overlap between your perspectives. If you share your friend's perspective on something, then you can both think the same way about it, even without talking.

This shared perspective builds the sense of connection between the two of you. You get the sense that you are seeing the world together, instead of individually.

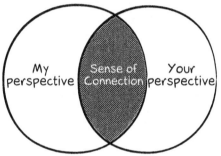

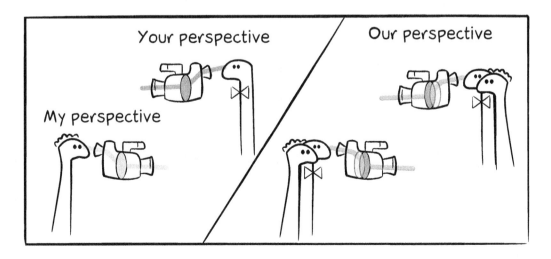

Accepting costs in a relationship

Nobody is perfect. Your friends, bosses, employees, teachers, and co-workers will always be a mix of good and bad.

This means that your relationship with them will provide you with some benefits but also some costs. As long as there are more benefits than costs, the relationship is good for you, and you should work at maintaining it.

This is especially important in a friendship. Nobody is all bad. Just because a friend has some faults, this doesn't mean you need to drop him/her as a friend.

If you expect your friends to accept your faults, then you must accept a few of theirs, too. This means putting up with the occasional bad mood, forgetfulness, and laziness. If it happens too often, then you can quietly talk to your friend about it, also inviting the friend to tell you what he/she wants you to change.

People assume

... that everyone likes being in a group.
Some people just like their groups to be small.

People expect

... that you know how to be a group member.
They expect you to blend in and cooperate.

4. Groups

People like being in groups. You've probably noticed that groups are everywhere: school and work teams, friendship groups and cliques, and gangs and clubs.

Belonging to groups is natural for human beings. Like other primates, human beings feel stronger and safer when they're in a group.

Why people want to be part of a group:

- **Emotions:** Loneliness is a very powerful emotion. People avoid loneliness by belonging to groups.

- **Needs:** People need to feel that they belong. They also need to feel loved, wanted, and respected. These needs can be fulfilled by a group.

- **Wants and fears:** People want safety and security. Living and working in groups helps people feel safe. As well, people who are insecure use groups to hide from their fears.

- **Identity:** People try to *be someone* by belonging to a group. They want to avoid *being a nobody*.

Costs and benefits of being in a group

For most people, the benefits of being in a group are larger than the costs. They feel happier being in a group than being alone.

The main cost is learning to get along with others. Since most people learn group skills as they grow up, this isn't usually a problem. If you never liked groups and played alone as a child, you might find group social skills a challenge.

However, it's impossible to avoid groups entirely. School, work, activities, and sports all involve groups. You can learn to manage groups if you keep these ideas in mind:

- **Costs and benefits:** Make yourself a benefit to the other group members, not a cost. People will like you more if you keep your costs to them low.

- **Wants, needs, and expectations:** Learn what the majority of people in the group want, need, and expect. When you fulfill these wants, needs, and expectations, you provide benefits to others.

- **Regular deposits:** To keep a group going, people have to work at the group relationship. Everyone expects each group member to help maintain the group. Make regular deposits of goodwill by doing your share of the work, helping out, listening, and cheerfully participating.

- **Shared perspective:** People in a group have spent time learning about the group's shared perspective. They know their common goals, ideas, and work. Learn about this shared perspective so that you can talk about or do the things that other people are interested in.

What to do

1 **Think about your costs and benefits to others in the group.**
Provide the group with benefits.

2 **Learn what they like and want.**
Fulfilling their expectations is a way of providing benefits.

3 **Find the shared perspective.**
Learn what interests others in the group.

Conforming to a group

Conforming means making yourself the same as or similar to other people in the group.

Most of the time, conforming just means finding the shared perspective of the group and adapting to it:

- **On a sports team:** *Is the shared goal to win, to get fit, or just to have fun?*

- **In a club:** *Are the shared interests based on activities or learning?*

- **In a social group:** *What interests does everyone have in common?*

When you know the shared perspective of the group, you can blend in.

But sometimes conforming means following the group's leaders so that everyone looks and acts the same. The leader guides (or manipulates) the group members into sameness.

Sometimes group members are the ones who put pressure on everyone to conform. They feel safer if everyone is the same.

Conformity for sameness and control is a cost to you, not a benefit. If you find the costs too high, then you might want to leave the group.

Easy groups and difficult groups

If you have difficulties with group social skills, you may want to spend your time with easy groups, rather than difficult groups.

Formal groups, such as clubs and community organizations, are the easiest to work with. The goals and common interests are usually spelled out in a document that you can take home and read. Joining the group is as easy as taking out membership and going to meetings. Because of the regular meetings, the carefully-explained shared perspective, and the need for new members, these groups tend to be more accepting of a wide variety of people, without expecting a lot of conformity.

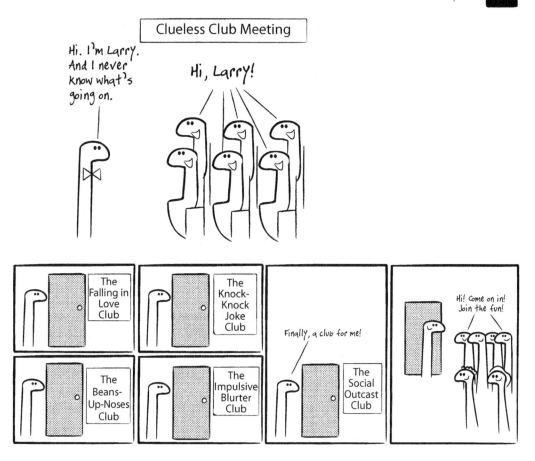

As a result, the benefits of formal groups are high, but the costs are low.

In contrast, informal groups, such as cliques and gangs, can be difficult to join. The expectations are never written down, and the pressure to conform is very high. These groups want only a certain kind of person as a member.

As a result, informal groups are high on costs and low on benefits.

5. Solving relationship problems

Do you know what to do when a problem occurs in a relationship? Maybe someone is angry. Maybe there's been a big misunderstanding.

Some people assume that if someone is angry, then the relationship is over. But no matter what the problem is, it can be fixed. Fixing relationship problems just takes a little effort. Don't throw out a relationship just because something is broken.

Why do relationship problems happen?

- **Withdrawals and costs:** One of you does something that subtracts a lot of goodwill from your relationship bank account. Then the other wonders if he/she should close the account.

- **Perspective problems:** Your likes and dislikes, wants, needs, and expectations are very different from your friend's. You do something that you consider a benefit, but the other person sees it as a cost—or vice versa.

The best way to start solving these relationship problems is to find out exactly what's wrong. And the easiest way is to just ask:

- *You seem upset. What's wrong? Is it something I did?*
- *I don't understand. Why exactly are you angry?*
- *I think we have a misunderstanding. Why don't you explain how you see it, then I'll explain how I see it?*

Once you start to talk, you can find out what's wrong, then make the right kinds of deposits to fix it. Saying nothing doesn't fix anything.

Ron felt helpless.

What had he done wrong? He and Ellen were talking by their lockers, and she was laughing and looked happy. Then suddenly, her smile disappeared. She frowned, said, "Never mind!" and then just walked off.

His anger boiled inside. But he realized that he was getting angry about something he didn't even understand. He needed to ask her what happened.

He found her later that day outside the gym. He waited till her friends left, feeling very nervous. Once she was alone, he walked up to her.

"Ellen? Sorry... I think I did or said something this morning that made you angry. Can we talk about it?"

Apologies

An apology fixes a low balance in a relationship. It lifts the account back up to the zero line. After that, you can make deposits to rebuild your relationship balance.

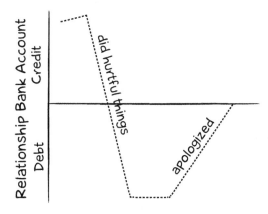

Get in the habit of apologizing whenever you realize you've made a withdrawal from the relationship, or when you notice you've created too many costs to the relationship.

Apologies feel awful. It's very humbling and embarrassing to say that you are in the wrong. Some people refuse to apologize because they want to avoid the feelings of apologies.

But that's exactly why apologies fix relationship problems. An apology has to be strong enough and meaningful enough to erase the damage. It can only have this kind of strength and meaning if you really mean it. So feeling horrible about apologizing is a sign that you're doing it right.

How to apologize:

- Don't wait. Do it right away.
- Use personal perspective. Think about what the person needs to hear you say. "*You are right. I owe you an apology. I let you down.*"
- Say what you did wrong. "*What I said was insensitive. I'm sorry.*"
- Don't try to deflect blame: "*It was my fault.*"
- If you are nervous, rehearse your apology in advance so that you know what you're going to say.
- Make amends. Tell the person how you're going to change or how you're going to fix the problem.
- Avoid written apologies. Do it face-to-face.
- Thank the person for listening, even if he/she is still angry. Everything kind you do will help the person cool down and forgive you, but maybe not right away.

What to do

1. **Be humble, not proud.**
   Say, "You are right. I owe you an apology."

2. **Take the blame.**
   Don't say it wasn't entirely your fault.

3. **Make amends.**
   Offer something more than just words.

4. **Thank the person for listening.**
   This thanks is your first deposit.

Mei cringed inwardly as she approached her sister.

She took a slow breath. "I'm sorry," she finally said. "I shouldn't have said what I said last night."

Her sister looked up from her book, surprised.

Mei continued. "It was my fault. I shouldn't have tried to blame you, especially in front of everybody else."

She paused, waiting for her sister to say something.

"So... am I forgiven?"

Her sister grinned. "Only if you go get me a chocolate milk from the kitchen."

"Done!" Mei ran off to the kitchen, relieved. Everything felt all right again.

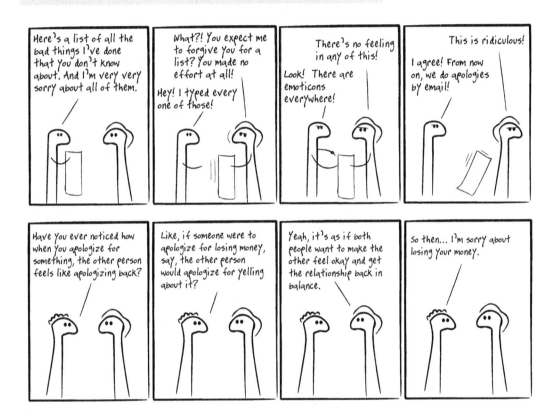

How not to apologize:

- **Built-in excuses:** An apology with built-in excuses is a fake apology. It starts with *"I'm sorry..."* and moves quickly to a second statement that undoes the apology. The person doesn't take full responsibility for the problem. This kind of "apology" isn't sincere and doesn't repair a relationship.

People expect

... that your apologies will be deep and sincere.

Otherwise, they will not repair the relationship.

- **Watered-down feelings:** People sometimes try to water down the apology to avoid feeling bad. They choose phrases like *sort of, maybe, a little bit*, etc., that don't take full blame. This weakens their apology.

    Well, maybe I'm kind of at fault here, if you look at it that way.

- **Double messages:** People use two different meanings of words in their apologies so that it sounds like an apology but really isn't. The phrase *I'm sorry* can mean *I apologize* but also *I'm sad about*. The following are fake apologies because they aren't actually apologizing for anything:

    I'm sorry you feel offended.

    I'm sorry that you misunderstood what I was saying.

- **Hidden insults:** When you avoid saying a real apology, you can end up accidentally insulting the person you're apologizing to. Think about your words from your listener's perspective before you speak. Does your apology sound more like an excuse? Does it suggest that the other person doesn't matter or is less important than you?

> **Rate These Apologies: Good or Bad?**
>
> _____ "I'm sorry that you feel that I should take more responsibility."
>
> _____ "I'm sorry. It's my fault. What I did was wrong."
>
> _____ "I'm sorry, but it wasn't really my fault."
>
> _____ "I'm sorry I ever decided to talk to you about anything!"
>
> _____ "I'm sorry that I offended you. My words came out wrong. I meant that I appreciate the effort you put into this."
>
> _____ "I'm sorry about the disaster in the kitchen. I've cleaned it up. Is there anything else I can do to make it up to you?"

Summary

Relationships are like bank accounts. If you want to keep your relationships, you need to keep your relationship bank accounts full.

- **Make regular deposits:** Good times, kindness, generosity, and responsibility keep your relationship alive. But acts of neglect, unkindness, self-centeredness, and irresponsibility drain your bank account.

- **Think about their wants, needs, and expectations:** People want different things from a relationship. Imagine someone's personal perspective to figure out what they would like from you.

- **Let friendships grow:** Close relationships take a long time to develop. They grow when you focus on building a shared perspective.

- **Adapt to group relationships:** Choose easy groups to join. Work at providing benefits to the group, not costs.

- **Solve relationship problems:** All relationship problems can be fixed. Ask what's wrong and learn to apologize to repair the damage.

Once you know what a relationship is and how to maintain it, you can work on your communication.

Chapter 6
Communication

Laura wasn't worried. She was a pro at apologizing.

"Sarah," she said with a warm smile, "I am very sorry about telling your secret earlier today."

"Really," Sarah said, not smiling.

Laura felt confident. This was going very well.

"Yep, I sure am." She flipped her hair back over her shoulder. "And I'd like to make amends."

"Really."

"Sure." Laura whipped out a pen and a notepad. "So, tell me... what kind of amends do you want?" She smiled up at Sarah again.

"Just one," Sarah said very quietly. She leaned over Laura. "To never have to listen to one of your stupid apologies again! And wipe that stupid smile off your face!"

What is communication?

Communication is more than just words. In fact, words are only ever a very small part of communication.

A much bigger part is *non-verbal* (or non-word) communication. People send messages with their voice, face, gestures, posture, clothes, timing, breathing, place, hands, actions, choices, priorities, and attitude.

If you pay attention only to messages that are in words, then you won't get all the messages. And if you aren't aware of the messages you are sending out, then you'll be constantly surprised by the way people respond to you.

Communication is like a SCENT.	Communication is any kind of message you send out, whether you intended it or not. What's important is whether **someone** received the message.

Words are only ever a small part of your message.

If you talk loudly, you communicate that you think you are important.

If you are smelly, you communicate that you don't care about other people's comfort.

You are communicating all the time.

You can think of communication the way you think about a resume. Part of the message in a resume is the words on the page. This is the *verbal* message. But another part of the message is in the document itself: the paper, colors, fonts, and details. Each of these communicates different *non-verbal* messages—ones that may even contradict the words themselves.

Tatters say: *"I don't care if I get this job."*

Coffee stains say: *"I didn't bother reprinting it."*

Spelling mistakes say: *"I'm careless."*

Resume of
Jake Doe

Education: HIgh School, Honor role

Work EXPerience: Various

Start Dat: AFter holidays

Resume of
Louise Doe

Education: High School Diploma

Work Experience: Summer Camp Counsellor :-)

Start Date: Whenever

Font choice says: *"I spend time on superficial things that are inappropriate."*

Emoticon says: *"I am silly and unprofessional."*

Vague slang says: *"I am flippant."*

Font choice says: *"I respect tradition and care about your expectations."*

Neatness says: *"I care about the quality of my work."*

Flexibility says: *"I will be an employee who adapts to your expectations."*

Resume of
Terry Doe

Education: High School Diploma, Honor roll

Work Experience: Grocery store clerk

Start Date: As soon as possible

People assume

... that you know your voice and body language are communicating messages. *Most of your message is in the way you say it.*

Basically, if your words say one thing but your voice, body language, style, and attitude say another, then nobody will believe your words. Messages from your voice and body are considered more honest than words.

1. Body language and voice

It's impossible to stop yourself from communicating non-verbally. Your brain triggers your body to show your thoughts and emotions, whether you want to or not.

This is why you'll see people using gestures when they're talking on the phone. They don't even realize they're doing it.

About 60 percent of your message comes from your face and body, and another 30 percent from the sound of your voice. Only 10 percent comes from your words. This is why you have to include emoticons in personal emails: otherwise, the other person would miss 90 percent of the message (and possibly get offended).

In face-to-face communication, anyone listening to you is paying far more attention to your voice and body language than to your words.

You can predict

1. **Does your appearance contradict your words?**
   People will believe your appearance.
2. **Does your voice contradict your message?**
   People will believe your voice.

Body language

Non-verbal communication is like an asterisk. In writing, you add an asterisk to a sentence to signal that there is a second explanation somewhere else on the page.

In speech, body language is like an asterisk on the spoken words. It means: *There's more to this communication than just my words. My body language reveals the real, hidden meaning.*

Your voice

The sound of your voice is like the font of your spoken words. People listen for sounds that communicate emotions.

Is your voice different from usual? Is it higher? Does that mean you're nervous? Is it louder or softer? More whiny? More tense?

Are you talking faster or more slowly than usual? More formally or less formally?

People know that these differences communicate your true feelings.

Managing your body language and voice

If you are aware of the messages from your body language and voice, then you can make your body and voice work with you, not against you.

- **Before you speak, decide what kind of overall message you want to give.** Do you want the listener to think you are lively and fun? Sober and serious? Authoritative? Kind?
- **Make yourself feel your message.** Make yourself feel lively and fun, or sober and serious, etc. This helps your brain create authentic body language and voice messages.
- **As you speak, assess yourself.** Does your voice and do your actions match your message? Adjust as you speak.
- **Watch how your listeners react.** Their voice and body language will communicate back to you whether they got your message, or whether they think something is odd.

What to do

1. **Choose what kind of message you want to communicate.**
   Confident? Kind? Strong?

2. **Feel that message.**
   When you feel it, your body and voice will communicate it.

3. **Listen to your voice.**
   Make it match your message.

4. **Watch other people's body language for feedback.**
   It will reveal what they are thinking about you.

- **Don't try to fake it:** Nothing is more obvious than fake body language. You have to really feel your message. If you don't feel it, then maybe that's not your real message anyway.

Silent signals

People also use body language to send silent messages to their friends. They use these silent signals when speaking out loud isn't allowed or when it's awkward or dangerous.

Never ignore silent signals. Some can save your life. Also never answer back out loud. There is always a good reason why people communicate silently.

If you can't figure out what the message means, keep watching quietly until you do. Or silently signal that you don't understand with a small shrug and raised eyebrows.

Communication   157

Examples of Silent Signals

Signal	Message
Your friend catches your eye and gives you a long, unsmiling look.	A warning. This could be a message that your friend is uncomfortable or nervous. Or it could be a signal to be silent and listen for danger. It could also be a signal to stop doing whatever you are doing because you're making people angry.
A non-friend catches your eye and gives you a long, unsmiling look.	A threat. Non-friends should not be sending you silent messages. You should probably think about getting out of that situation.
Your friend jerks his/her chin while catching your eye.	Pointing. Follow the direction of the chin to see what he/she is pointing at, then check back with your friend to make sure you're looking at the right thing. Think about the context to decode the signal.
Your friend's eyes widen suddenly.	A shocked stop message. You may have just said something harmful or embarrassing. Stop what you are doing or saying. Check your friend's body language to see if he/she looks relieved.
Your friend raises his/her eyebrows while catching your eye.	

2. A smile as a message

A smile is instinctive communication. It's a signal of reassurance. It means everything is okay.

You use a smile when you're giving a good-news message. If there is no smile, people don't know if everything is okay, and your message just becomes confusing, like the "happy face" beside this paragraph.

It's important to remember to smile when you give these types of messages:

- **Greetings:** The smile tells people that they are welcome. Without it, they would feel as if they're intruding.

- **Requests:** Smile when you say *excuse me* or *please* or when you're making a request, so that the other person knows you're not trying to be pushy. Without the smile, the other person might get angry.

- **Introductions:** Smiling at someone you are just meeting communicates that you are willing to like that person. Without the smile, your new acquaintance would feel offended.

- **Thanks:** Smile when you say *thank you* to add feeling to your words. Without the smile, the other person will assume you don't mean it.

It's important to avoid smiling in the following situations, because you will give the wrong message:

- **Apologies:** A smile makes you appear insincere. You don't want your apology to look like a joke.

- **Confusion:** A smile makes you appear to know what you're doing. If you're confused, don't smile out of nervousness. Keep your face looking serious or concerned, and ask for help.

- **With unfamiliar people:** A smile has to match your familiarity with someone. With strangers, your smile should be very short and polite. Too much smile to a stranger will creep the person out because you are being too friendly. (But if you don't give enough of a smile to a good friend, that friend will be offended because you're being too cold.)

People expect

... that you will smile if your message is good news.
Otherwise, they will assume it's bad news.

3. Silence as a message

Silence is the absence of speech, but not the absence of communication. People communicate through silence the way they communicate through body language.

A silence rarely means nothing at all. To avoid embarrassing mistakes, always figure out what the silence means before you interrupt it.

Context clues:

Silence gets most of its meaning from the context:

- **Place:** Is this a place where people expect others to be silent (such as a movie theater or a class)? Is it full of people who are trying to concentrate (such as an exam)? Is there an event taking place that calls for periods of silence (such as a funeral)?

- **Time:** What happened just before the silence? Was it shocking or surprising? Are people waiting for someone to answer or act? What's going to happen next that is making people go silent?

- **Situation:** What is happening? Is the silence in anticipation of what's coming? Is there something happening nearby that people are listening to?

- **People:** Are you talking about something that someone might find offensive? Did someone enter the room who should not hear what you are saying? Are the people around you feeling upset or angry about something you (or someone else) said or did? Are you supposed to be the listener, not the talker?

Avoid thinking "nobody minds" if nobody says anything. Silence is often a *stop* signal. If the person's body language is grim and stiff, and especially if the person is trying to catch your eyes, then you can conclude that the silence means *stop*.

Examples of different types of silence:

- **Frosty silence:** A polite but icy silence, often with a tight-lipped, fake smile. It communicates disapproval, usually from someone older than you.

- **Shocked silence:** A mid-conversation stop that communicates shock or embarrassment at something someone has said.

- **Clingy silence:** A person wants attention but is reluctant to ask for it, and hangs around silently nearby waiting for you to notice.

- **Emotional silence:** A silence when someone is too emotional to reply. The person is close to tears or anger and cannot form words.

- **Respectful silence:** Refraining from talking to show respect for and sympathy with someone's pain or sadness.

- **Pregnant pause:** The silence that comes after a question and before the answer because the answer is negative.

- **Awkward silence:** A break in a light conversation because the topic ran out. Someone usually makes a joke to break the awkwardness.

- **Silent answer:** A refusal to respond to or make eye contact with you because you're supposed to be paying attention, not talking.

- **Alert silence:** A sudden stiffening of the body because someone heard something hidden or faraway and wants to alert you to it.

- **Comfortable silence:** Walking or working side-by-side with a close friend and not feeling the need to say anything.

4. Eye connection

Your eyes show better than any other part of your body what you are thinking.

Remember that for road safety, it's important to lock eyes with drivers. When you see people's eyes, you get a good idea what they're thinking. Also, people usually look in the direction they are about to move.

Similarly, people communicate their thoughts and intentions with their eyes, whether they realize it or not. This is why most people watch other people's eyes by instinct. Glancing often at people's eyes helps you stay aware of what they're thinking.

What is eye contact?

Eye contact does not mean looking directly into someone's eyes. That kind of eye contact feels embarrassing. Besides, people have two eyes, so you would only be able to look at one eye at a time.

Eye contact really means:

- **Checking the face around the eyes and the mouth:** This is where most facial expressions show. Since facial expressions show emotions, they communicate what people are thinking.

- **Being able to see the other person's eyes:** When you see someone's eyes, you can see what he/she is looking at. People tend to look at the things they are thinking about.

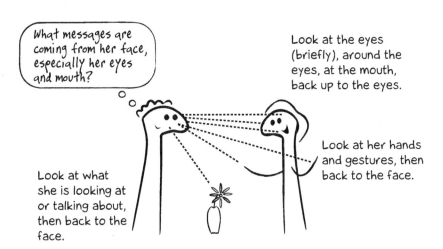

What to do

1. **Glance at the face around the eyes and mouth.**
   Look for tiny changes in expression that signal a change in thought or mood.

2. **Check for approval.**
   Smiles, nods, and relaxed looks signal approval.

3. **Watch for silent eye signals.**
   Respond silently.

4. **Follow their gaze.**
   People look at what they are thinking about.

The purpose of eye contact

The purpose of eye contact is to *search for communication*. It's not about staring. Eye contact that is posed and artificial won't do you any good.

In eye contact, your eyes flit around the face, looking for signals. They center on the eyes and mouth because tiny changes in facial expressions there carry big meanings.

Messages to look for:

- **Approval:** Glancing at people's eyes helps you see their reactions to the things you say and do. Their faces should look reasonably happy and should be looking at yours.

- **Silent signals:** Sometimes people communicate with their eyes. They might communicate *Don't do that* or *Sh, we're playing a joke, don't let on.* Or even *Quiet! I think we're being followed!* By glancing at a person's eyes often, you'll receive these important silent messages.

- **Changes:** Facial expressions change if emotions change. You can see these changes only if you have been paying attention to their face.

- **Gaze:** You can follow a person's gaze to see what he/she is looking at. This tells you what he/she is thinking about.

- **Mood:** The person's face reveals how he/she is feeling. You will see fatigue, hunger, desperation, boredom, and other feelings only if you are looking at his/her face. When you know someone's mood, you can predict his/her emotional reaction to the things you say and do.

5. People reading you

You are communicating all the time, so people are "reading" you all the time.

Why? Because people are naturally curious. They want to know what's going on in your head. They want to be able to predict how you're going to react. So they spend a lot of time observing you and reading your communication.

Is this creepy? Not really. You do it too. By constantly reading the people around you, you get the information you need to get along with everybody.

People assume

... that your body language and voice communicate your real message.

They think you are aware what messages you're sending out.

Examples of reading body language:

- *There's Luke. He looks as if he just got out of bed. I wonder if he was out late last night.*

- *Did Louise just catch Jake's eye? Does this mean "I told you so"?*

- *Sam's looking around the room and fidgeting. I think he's nervous. He says he feels calm, but I don't believe that for a minute.*

- *Theo looks angry, but he says he's fine. Is he contradicting himself on purpose? Or is he lying or hiding something? Or maybe playing a trick?*

- *Mom says she doesn't mind if I go out tonight. But she said it very oddly, and her expression didn't match her words. Is she angry about something?*

- *Pau's voice sounds hard when he says he loves me. His eyes look annoyed. I think he wants to break up with me.*

People also read your actions, choices, and attitude. What you choose to do (out of all the choices you could make) communicates what you really think. People combine these observations with your voice and body language and come to conclusions.

Examples of reading choices and actions:

- *Mark left the meeting early again. He's always leaving early. That means he doesn't care.*

- *Pam forgets her lunch a lot and bums food off the rest of us. She just thinks she can get away with a free lunch every day!*

- *I would never be late for a meeting unless there was an emergency. So if Ted is late every day, that means he just isn't trying very hard.*

- *Lisa chose Jen to be her partner. She didn't even look at me. She must like Jen better than she likes me.*

Communication   **165**

How People Read You

What they see	What they assume
You missed two practices for the soccer tryouts. You say you forgot.	You don't really want to make the team. You just want everyone to think you do.
You always forget to bring your share of the work to the lab group, even when everyone calls you to remind you.	You're lazy. Or you don't care. Or you haven't even done the work but don't want everyone to know.
You complained that you didn't want to do the dishes. Then you accidentally dumped all the dish soap down the drain.	

How to read people

You read people all the time too. But are you good at it? Do you come to a lot of false conclusions? Here are some steps for reading someone's non-verbal communication.

- **Figure out the person's baseline state.** The baseline state is how a person is normally, such as when the person is relaxed. Observe and remember how he/she looks, talks, and acts when not much is going on.

- **Note any deviations:** When the person's non-verbal communication changes from the usual baseline state, you know that the person's thoughts and feelings have changed. Notice these changes.

- **Interpret the meaning of the changes:** Figure out the reason for the changes. *What has just happened? What is about to happen? Who just entered the room? Who left? Who said something important?* Look for context clues to help you identify the right reason.

What to do

1. **Learn their baselines.**
   Observe them in their relaxed state.

2. **Notice deviations.**
   Compare changes back to the baseline.

3. **Figure out a reason for the change.**
   Get clues from the context.

4. **Compare their actions to yourself and to others.**
   People act fairly similarly when they have the same thoughts and feelings.

- **Compare to yourself:** Compare someone's body language, voice, and actions to how you would behave (or are behaving) in the same situation. Ask yourself: *When I look like that, what's the reason? Is it because I am angry? Nervous? Confused?* Think about how you feel when you do those actions or say those words. You can assume that the other person is not very different from you.

- **Compare to others:** You can also compare someone's body language, voice, and actions to how others in the same situation are behaving. When people have similar thoughts and feelings, they have similar body language, voice, and other non-verbal communication. But if someone's non-verbal communication is noticeably different than everyone else's, then you can conclude that that person has thoughts and feelings that are different from everyone else's.

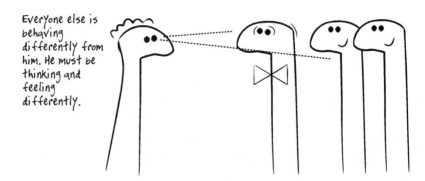

6. First impressions

Non-verbal communication is very important in first impressions. A person you're meeting for the first time doesn't know you and doesn't know your baselines. So he/she forms conclusions based only on what he/she sees right now.

Strangers read you and size you up quickly. They look at all your communication and ask themselves: *What is this telling me? What does it look like to me?*

Strangers assume

... that your non-verbal communication is accurate.
They believe you are aware what messages you are sending out.

Communication from your appearance:

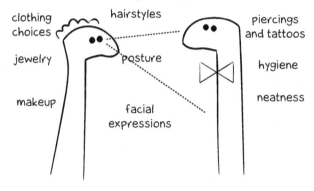

Communication from your voice:

Communication from your conversation:

As well, strangers observe your actions and choices and read them. They believe that through your actions and choices, you're trying to show them what you think.

Jill sat nervously as the interviewer sorted his papers. She was tempted to just start talking, but she knew that was just her nerves. She didn't want to give this guy the impression that she was a chatterbox.

"So, tell me about yourself," the interviewer finally said. "Tell me why you're interested in this job."

Jill was glad she'd prepared an answer for this question! She didn't want to ramble on and on, giving the impression that she was unfocused.

"I'm a recent graduate with 12 years of experience working in retail and in design projects. I'm interested in this job because it includes both retail and design. I like working at the things I'm good at." She smiled to the interviewer to communicate that she meant what she said.

"Does this mean you don't like doing new things?"

"Oh, not at all," Jill said quickly, shaking her head slightly to emphasize her message. "I just want to get off to a good start first so that the company will have confidence in me."

How to manage first impressions

Managing first impressions is a skill. Here are some ideas for learning to manage first impressions well.

- **See yourself from the perspective of others:** Imagine a camera pointed at you. What would it see and hear?

- **Be polite, cheerful, and warm:** Avoid strong emotions and strong opinions till the person gets to know you well.

- **Let the other person decide what you'll talk about:** Listen and ask questions. Find topics the other person seems to find interesting. Avoid talking about yourself. Show genuine curiosity.

- **Find your shared perspective with that person:** When you talk about interests you have in common, you won't be nervous. Your non-verbal communication will be more natural and relaxed.

What to do

1. See yourself from the stranger's perspective.
   Pretend you've never met yourself before.

2. Act and talk like others.
   Try to blend in.

3. Find your shared perspective with that person.
   Your body language will become more relaxed and happy.

Reading surroundings

Strangers don't just read you; they also read your surroundings. Your surroundings tell them a lot about who you are and what you think about.

Is your workplace neat or messy? Are there fresh flowers or plants? Photos of friends or children? Clocks, timers, calendars, and agenda books? Items that show a sense of humor?

Is your home grand or modest? Tidy or messy? Stylish, artistic, homey, or dowdy? Full of books, games, magazines, or hobby items?

When people meet you for the first time, they're trying hard to figure out who you are. You might think they base most of their conclusions on your voice, body language, appearance, actions, and choices—and you're right. But once they see your dorm room, locker, or work desk, they often revise their conclusions.

Manage these first impressions by thinking about the message your surroundings give. Should you clean and vacuum before your new friend visits? Should you rearrange your office space to get rid of clutter before the boss drops by?

Summary

Communication is more than just words; it's everything that goes along with the words:

- **Body language and voice:** Your body language and voice communicate your thoughts and feelings more than your words. People tend to believe your non-verbal communication more than your words.

- **Smiles:** Smiles communicate that everything is okay. Smile when you give good-news messages; otherwise, you'll confuse your listeners.

- **Silence:** Silence is communication. Use the context to figure out what a silence means.

- **Eye contact:** Use your eyes to search someone's face for expressions, emotions, and small changes. Eye contact is not about staring—look just enough to stay aware of his/her feelings.

It's important to understand that people watch for your non-verbal communication. They pick up on messages, even if you didn't intend to send them out.

- **People are always reading you:** See yourself from their perspective to make sure they make the right conclusions about you.

- **People base first impressions on non-verbal communication:** Strangers size you up very quickly. Small gestures, expressions, and voice changes make a big impact on strangers. Think about your non-verbal communication when you are with strangers.

Good communication skills are the foundation of a slightly more complex application of common sense—*conversation*.

Chapter 7
Conversation

Will listened to everyone chatting

for a while. Everyone was joking around and laughing. He could do that too.

"Did you hear the one about the drunken shepherd taking ballet lessons?" he called out with a grin, pushing toward the center of the group.

Silence greeted him.

He pressed on. "There was this shepherd who drank too much. And one day he—"

He felt a jab in the ribs. His friend Tony had elbowed him.

"What?" Will growled.

Tony just gave a tight-lipped smile, then looked at someone else. "So, you were saying, Lee?"

Will couldn't believe how rude Tony was being, cutting him off like that. He shoved his way out of the group and left.

What is conversation?

Conversation is not about words and talking. It's not even about communication.

Conversation is about relationships. Surprised? People converse to build relationships with each other. And like relationships, conversation is about the connections they make, not about the information they tell.

The Latin roots *con-* and *verse-* mean *to turn together*. A conversation goes well when everyone is thinking about the other people and "turning together."

Conversation is like an ENGINE. 	Engines are made up of parts that work together. Each part depends on other parts to keep it going. 
Timing and fit are important. If parts move too fast or too slow, or if they are too big or too small to fit the other parts, then the engine will grind to a halt. 	In a conversation, each person is a part in the conversation's engine. 
A conversation doesn't dump words and ideas on people. Everyone's words and ideas work together. 	**Conversation is about relationships, not about words**

1. Conversation and people

Conversation isn't about telling people what you think. It's about learning things about other people.

What are you discovering?

- **Personality:** how similar or different someone is from you
- **Interests:** how much that person's interests overlap with yours and how much he/she is unique and different.
- **Connections:** how many friends, places, and experiences you have in common

Basically what you're trying to discover is your *shared perspective*. Conversations search for, find, and explore the shared perspectives of all the people talking. The talking is just there to help uncover that shared perspectives. The more you learn about each other, the more you can talk about.

Talking with vs. talking at

Sure, some people talk only from their own perspective. They talk about things the other person doesn't even care about, often for a long time. This is often called *talking at* someone.

Talking at someone isn't a conversation because it doesn't focus on the relation-

What to do

1. **Focus on the person, not the words.**
   Conversation is about relationships.

2. **Find topics you're both interested in.**
   Find and explore your shared perspective.

3. **Ask questions.**
   Let the other person talk while you listen.

Talking at

People assume

... that you want to talk with them, not at them.

They want to find your shared perspective together.

ship. In fact, talking at someone is a kind of insult, because it suggests that the person is there just to be listening box.

In real conversation, people talk in their shared perspective. They build connections with other people by exchanging ideas. This is called *talking with* other people.

Talking with

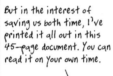

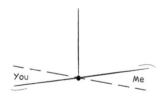

2. Conversation and equality

Conversation belongs equally to you and to the other person (or people). It's impossible to share perspectives if one person talks all the time. Good conversation is balanced; it gives everyone time to talk and time to listen.

Balanced conversation focuses on everyone present. Everyone has opportunities to talk and to listen. Everyone is trying to learn about the persective of the others.

Being the center of attention is a sign that you are not allowing everyone to share the conversation. When you talk more than your share, people think you are self-centered. They may even conclude that you are bragging.

Conversations are balanced when they focus on every person in the group equally. If you are in a two-person conversation, you get to talk no more than half the time. If it's a five-person conversation, you get to talk one-fifth of the time.

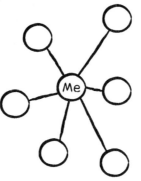

Me-Centered Conversation

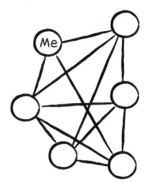

Balanced Conversation

Louis wanted to say more, but he knew he'd already talked his share.

So he listened. His four friends were talking about their digital cameras, and by far, he had the best-quality camera in the group. He'd also taken courses in digital editing. He wanted to talk, but he forced himself to listen instead.

Jennie mentioned some photos she'd submitted to a photo contest. That was interesting. Was Jennie a hobby photographer, just like him? He was curious about this possible new connection.

"What kinds of shots did you send in?" he asked.

"Oh, some that I shot with my telephoto in the backyard," she answered.

Telephoto? Then she was a far more serious photographer than he'd realized.

Louis was glad he'd been listening instead of talking, because now he'd discovered a new connection.

How to make people feel good

In relationships, people like you based on how you make them feel. The same is true for conversation. If your conversation makes people feel happy, relaxed, and respected, they'll like you and enjoy talking to you.

What to do

1. **Share the conversation.** Help everyone feel equal.
2. **Listen and ask questions.** You want to show that you're interested.
3. **Focus on making people feel good.** Fun, good times, laughter, respect, and good listening make people feel good about you.

What makes people feel good:

- **Genuine listening and interested questions:** *I can't believe you did that. Was it scary?*

- **Encouragement, smiles, and compliments:** *You're good that this, so I think you should have the first turn.*

- **Exploring things in common:** *You're from up north? Me too. What school did you go to?*

- **Fun and laughter:** *If I tell you how I goofed that up, will you promise not to laugh? You probably will anyway!*

- **Feeling comfortable and respected:** *Sorry, it's your turn. I interrupted. Go ahead.*

- **Avoiding hurtful comments**

Yabbut conversations

A yabbut conversation makes people feel bad. Instead of agreeing, you start every sentence with "Yeah, but" to argue every statement the other person makes:

"Yeah, but reality shows are just fake."

"Yeah, but everybody knows they're just acting."

This doesn't build connections with that person. It suggests that you aren't listening or trying to understand. It's also kind of insulting, like a put-down.

What should you say when you want to talk but you have an opposite opinion? Instead of arguing, start with a point you agree on, then phrase your ideas as a question:

"I like the tension in reality shows too. Do you ever wonder how much of it's rehearsed and edited?"

"I watched that show too! What did you think when the group leader said he wanted to leave? Did it sound fake to you? I didn't believe him."

3. Conversation and personal perspectives

What do people like most in a conversation? They like when you and others talk about the things they're interested in.

People see the world through their personal perspective. Whatever's going on inside their heads affects how they react to your conversation. So talking about things in a way that they like and understand is going to be more successful than talking just any old way.

Here are some ideas for adapting your conversation to your listeners' perspectives:

- **Consider his/her priorities:** Have you ever tried to talk to someone who had something else on his/her mind? He/she probably couldn't concentrate on what you're saying. The only way to get someone to connect with you is to talk about his/her priorities. If you talk about something different, then your listener will just get annoyed.

- **Adapt to his/her education and background:** Not everyone has the same education and experiences as you. When you're talking to people who don't know what you know, talk in words they'll understand. Consider their personal perspective so that you can accurately guess what words they like and understand. Otherwise, you won't be able to connect or communicate.

- **Consider memories and experiences:** Remember the experience lens? People associate words with their memories and experiences. A word that seems neutral to you can be emotional to someone else. A word that means something good to you can mean something bad to someone else. Consider someone's memories and experiences when choosing your words.

"Happy Valentines Day!" Eve called out to her friend Bette.

Bette scowled. "Don't tell me to have any happy stupid Valentines Day!"

"What's with you?"

"You know I don't have a boyfriend," Bette said. "Valentine's Day is kind of pointless if you're not in a relationship. It's stupid, really. Who wants to be reminded that everyone else is in love except me?"

"I never thought of it like that." Eve grew thoughtful for a moment. "I guess it would be kind of like someone wishing me a Happy Employee Day."

"Considering that you got laid off last week," Bette said. "Yes, it's like that. We have to think of the other person's experiences before we say something to them to avoid these awkward situations!"

Personal perspective and misunderstandings

If two people are speaking English together, then they're speaking the same language. Right?

Not necessarily. Even though the dictionary defines what

words mean, people have very different *personal* meanings for the words they use.

For example, if you use the phrase *on time*, you may mean *no more than five minutes late*. But your friend might think that *on time* means *no more than thirty minutes late*. Someone else might think it means *not late at all*. These differences in personal meaning can create a lot of confusion and frustration!

Abstract words like *truth*, *democracy*, *justice*, and *fairness* can have very different meanings for different people and in different situations.

How to speak the same language

Arguments occur when people use the same words to mean different things. To avoid problems with word meanings, try the following:

- **Use simple words:** Use short, common words that everybody understands: *Cut round holes big enough to let thick oil through.* Don't try to use big or complicated words: *Create circular apertures of sufficient diameter to permit the passage of lubricant of high viscosity.*

- **Use short sentences:** Simple grammar makes your meaning easier to understand: *Let's leave early. I'd rather not be late.* instead of: *I think we should probably strive not to be late, since we all remember what happened last time, so we should think about leaving on the early side.*

- **Consider the context:** Could the current context affect how people understand your meaning? If it's in the evening, don't just say *we'll meet at 8:00*. Some people might assume it's *p.m.*, others *a.m.*

- **Explain unusual or abstract words**: If you need to use an unusual word (*paradigm*) or an abstract word (*leadership*), consider explaining what you mean by it.

- **Ask:** If someone argues with you or reacts strangely to what you said, assume that you have different personal meanings for some of the key words. Talk about the possible differences in meaning to help avoid an argument: *I wonder if we both mean the same thing when we say we'll do it soon. What amount of time do you mean?*

What to do

1. **Think about the other person's perspective.**
   This helps you match your conversation to their needs, priorities, and experiences.

2. **Speak plainly.**
   Avoid phrases that can have personal meanings.

3. **Use simple grammar.**
   If you keep it short and to the point, more people will understand.

"I hate him!"

"Who?" Jay asked.

"My missing-in-action boyfriend!" Allie glowered. "The no-good creep!"

Jay frowned. This didn't make sense. The last time he saw Allie and Ron together, they were very close—and that was just yesterday. "Why do you, um, hate him?"

"He hasn't called me all day! I've left at least 50 messages! If he's going to dump me, he should just come and do it to my face!"

> Jay shook his head. Hard. "Allie, weren't you listening yesterday when he told us all that he was going to Mexico for two weeks? He even said good-bye to you."
>
> She looked astonished. "Mexico? Two weeks? Really?"
>
> "Yeah. He's not around. So he can't call you."
>
> "I guess I'm not the world's greatest listener..."
>
> "I guess not."
>
> Then Allie gave Jay a quick hug and grinned. "Oh, I love him!"
>
> "But just a minute ago you said you hated him!"
>
> "You knew I didn't mean it that way!"

4. Group conversations

When you're having a conversation with just one person, you often have a large shared perspective with that person.

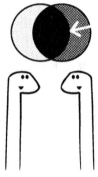

But in a group conversation, everyone has a different perspective. The overlap of everyone's perspectives is usually fairly small. Even if you are all in the same club or hobby, you may find that the activity itself is the only thing you have in common.

For this reason, groups usually talk about light and casual topics, such as events, food, sports, entertainment, work, and hobbies.

Having a serious conversation with a group is difficult. It's too hard to find something to talk about that everybody understands and that doesn't offend anyone. Usually it's best to save serious talk for one-on-one conversations.

Small talk

A lot of people say they're not good at small talk. They mean that small talk makes them feel awkward.

Sure, it's hard to find the right topics to keep a conversation going when you don't know the people well or you aren't supposed to talk about anything serious.

But the point of small talk is not to be a great verbal acrobat. And it's not about wasting time and breath either! It's about *maintaining relationships* and *finding shared perspectives*—the same as for any conversation. If you keep this in mind, you'll find that small talk becomes easier.

Small talk with people you have just met

Small talk with people you have just met is always light conversation. You don't know about your shared perspective yet, so you can't talk deeply about anything. You also don't know this person enough to know what topics are sensitive, embarrassing, or annoying to this person, so you want to keep the conversation cautious and safe.

Start the conversation with something from your context: the place, the day, the situation, or the people. These topics are reasonably safe because they are all around you.

> *What a great place!*
>
> *How do you know Mark?*
>
> *Were you at the game this morning?*

As you start talking, you'll gradually discover things in common. Then you can ask questions on those topics.

What to do

1. **Make the person feel comfortable.**
   Be warm and polite, and respect their familiarity level with you.

2. **Start with context topics.**
   Talk about place, time, situation, and people topics till you discover common interests.

3. **Watch body language.**
   People use non-verbal communication to show when they are uncomfortable.

Keep in mind that you're not *familiar* with new acquaintances. For this reason, your conversation shouldn't be overly friendly or close. People get freaked out when a stranger becomes too friendly too quickly.

Tips for small talk with people you've just met:

- **Be warm and polite:** You want them to like you, not be surprised or shocked by you.

- **Talk about things in the context:** Start a conversation by talking about the place or event, the people who invited you, or things that happened that day. Avoid opinion topics or heavy subjects.

- **Look for your shared perspective:** When you discover things you have in common, ask questions to explore them further.

- **Don't be overwhelming:** New acquaintances are not the same as close friends. They don't know you. Watch for non-verbal communication that suggests that the person is uncomfortable, bored, or unhappy.

Small talk with friends

With friends you know well, you can have deeper conversation. But sometimes you don't. Sometimes friends just want to chat about nothing at all.

Small talk with friends is usually just slang greetings, comments, jokes, and light talk about the things going on around you.

Lots of smiles and laughs, nothing more.

Why talk about nothing? Remember that small talk among friends is really about relationships. Talking about nothing often says lots about relationships. It can say:

> "You're still my friend. You're important enough to me that I want to talk to you, even if there's nothing much to talk about."

> "Our shared perspective is fun. We can just enjoy it without saying much."

> "I want you to have fun when you're with me. So let's keep this light and silly."

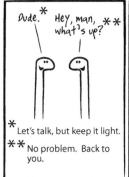

Small talk with friends:

- **Focus on your relationships:** Think about the people, not the talk. You are trying to build and maintain your connection with these friends.

- **Listen for the rhythm:** Is the conversation all short sentences? Jokes and laughs? Is everyone using slang? Keep the same rhythm when you join in.

- **Let the group set the topics:** If you're not good at small talk, let someone else lead. In small talk, topics change quickly, so keep your contributions short and listen for changes.

- **Be positive:** Small talk among friends is cheerful. The goal is to make people feel good. Don't change the subject to something more serious.

- **Don't look for content:** Small talk with friends is usually about nothing. There is no topic. Avoid trying to turn a comment into a topic.

What to do

1. **Focus on the people.**
   Use small talk to build up your connections with them.

2. **Follow the rhythm.**
   Stick to the topics, follow the changes, and keep it simple.

3. **Be fun.**
   People like to talk to people who make them feel good.

Beware of brain droppings

Do you have ideas flitting around in your head all the time? So does everybody else. But do you always say them out loud?

Just because an idea is in your head, that doesn't mean you should say it. Is it relevant to other people's perspective? Does it make sense in the conversation? Or is it just clutter?

Brain droppings are annoying. If you have a habit of blurting whatever is in your head, get a Twitter account. Then people can read your brain droppings when they are interested in them.

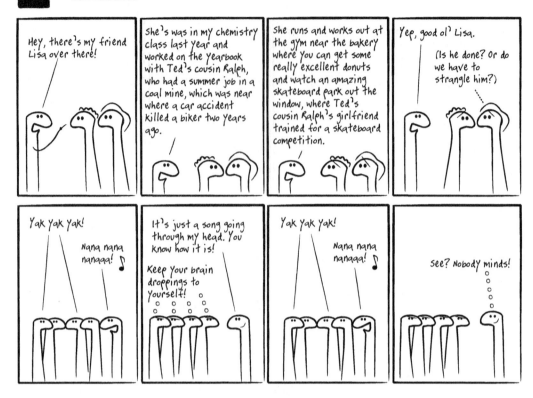

Dealing with boredom

Sometimes a conversation gets boring. But standing around looking bored will not add to your relationship accounts with anyone. Sighing, shifting from one foot to another, or staring off into space will all be insulting to the people around you.

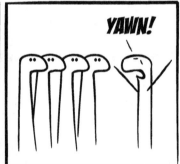

What to do:

- **Wait it out:** In most group conversations, the topic changes a lot, so you won't have to wait long till there is a new topic.

- **Focus on relationships:** Use the opportunity to learn about the people you are with. What are they revealing about their personal perspectives? Watch their non-verbal communication to improve how well you read people.

- **Give yourself a learning goal:** Even in a boring topic, there is always something worth learning. Can you learn the vocabulary of this sport? The plot line of this television show? Some technical details about how something works? You never know when this learning will be useful.

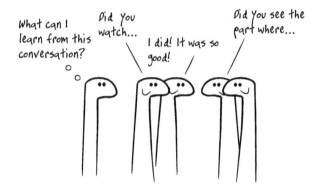

Will stifled a yawn.

How long were they going to talk about their part-time jobs? Will didn't have a job. His hobby of creating digital animations took up all his time, so he wasn't really interested.

Still, he tried to give himself a learning goal. Could he learn about the types of jobs available in town? He decided to give it a try.

He listened for a few minutes. Then he asked Kara and Jennie how long it took them to find their jobs. And he asked Ben if he liked his boss. It was all mildly interesting, and he learned a lot about his friends.

Then out of the blue, Larry said something about how he'd heard that someone at Digital Creations was looking for a part-timer to help with animation programming.

Will couldn't believe his ears. A perfect job for him?

Later, after he'd called Digital Creations and set up an interview, he texted Larry: "How come you never told me about this before?"

"You never seemed interested in jobs before," Larry replied.

What to do

1. **Avoid looking bored.**
   That will damage your relationships.

2. **Give yourself a learning goal.**
   Find something useful or interesting in the topic.

3. **Wait for a topic change.**
   Conversation topics change often.

People assume

... that you care about your listeners.
They believe you want them to be happy.

5. Four unwritten rules of conversation

1. The permission rule

This rule says that *you need to get your listener's permission to talk*. You are not allowed to continue talking unless you get that permission.

Why? Because everyone is forced to listen to everything you say. So they should have a say in what they have to put up with.

And they do. Listeners contribute to the conversation by giving the talker *permission signals*. Permission signals tell the talker to continue talking. When the talker stops getting these permission signals, he/she must stop talking and let someone else take over.

Remember this when you are the listener. Giving permission signals is a very important part of the conversation.

Examples of permission signals:

- nods
- smiles
- laughs
- warm eye contact
- murmurs of surprise
- questions
- comments
- leaning forward
- tilting head
- eyebrow movements

Examples of no-permission signals:

- silence
- no smile
- no response
- looking away
- interrupting
- frowns and tight lips
- catching someone's eye
- shifting from foot to foot
- shaking head
- loud sighs

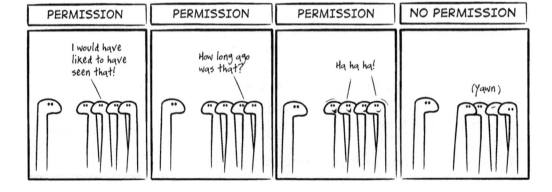

2. The one-sentence rule

This rule says that in a conversation, *you are permitted to offer just one sentence at a time*. You need to get permission before you offer another sentence.

Why? Because conversation is not an opportunity to make a speech, or even to talk in paragraphs. The rhythm is

Sentence   Permission   Sentence   Permission

Remember: the permission can be as simple as a smile, nod, or eye contact. Your listener may even provide the permission *while you are talking*. But without a clear permission signal, you have to stop talking. You've lost the connection with the other person.

Why people deny permission to continue

Listeners sometimes refuse to give you a permission signal to continue. This means that your conversation isn't working.

- **Boredom:** The topic is outside the shared perspective of the group. The listeners aren't interested.
- **Discomfort:** The topic is private, controversial, or insulting to some members of the group. By stopping you, the listeners are saving you from embarrassment.
- **Hurt:** The topic is painful to some members of the group. By stopping you, the listeners are preventing you from hurting someone.
- **Misunderstanding:** What you said wasn't clear, so your listeners didn't understand and have moved on. You may have another chance to try again later. But for now, let someone else talk.

People expect

... that you will keep your conversations equal.
Listeners get to choose what they want to listen to.

People assume

... that conversation hogs are self-centered.

They don't understand why anyone would talk in paragraphs.

3. The no-hogging rule

This rule says that nobody owns a conversation, not even the person who started it. *Never use a conversation to give lectures or speeches or to tell long stories without giving people a chance to respond.*

Why? Because conversations have to be equal and balanced. If you don't balance your talking and listening, then you communicate that you think you're more important than everyone else. This harms your relationships.

Besides, people don't like to be bullied and dominated. They don't like being forced to listen. They want the conversation to be for them, too.

If you follow the one-sentence rule and get permission before continuing, then you are unlikely to become a conversation hog. If someone changes the topic before you get to say all you wanted to say, let it go. You do not have permission to continue. Maybe you can tell your story some other day.

Hogging habits

- **The um habit:** Some people have a habit of saying *um* at the end of every sentence. This *um* communicates *I have more to say, so don't cut in.* Using *um* at the end of every sentence may seem to allow you to string many sentences together; but you are holding your listeners hostage, and they won't like that.

- **The rising intonation habit:** Some people raise their voice at the end of every sentence, as if it's a question. This makes every sentence sound unfinished. The listeners are forced by politeness not to cut in. So the person continues rambling while the listeners become more annoyed and frustrated.

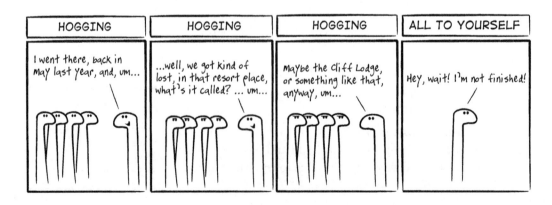

4. The topic-change rule

Conversations don't stay on the same topic for very long. This rule says that *when the topic changes, everyone must follow the topic change.*

Why? Because a conversation is not like an essay or speech. It doesn't have a beginning, middle, and end. It is a continuous flow of topics and ideas.

Fighting a topic change is like swimming against the current of a river. It rarely works. Besides, fighting a topic change communicates that you are more interested in yourself and your ideas than you are in the people around you. This damages your relationships.

What if you still had more to say when the topic changed? Everyone else had more to say too. Your job in a conversation is not to exhaust the topic but to maintain your relationships.

Whatever is unsaid gets left behind. That is topic material for another time.

Fighting a topic change

Here are some ways people try to fight topic changes:

- **Backpedalling:** Some people don't like leaving a topic "unfinished." They try to stop the new topic and drag the conversation back to the old topic. But this will fail because people won't follow.

- **Ignoring a new topic:** Sometimes a topic comes up that doesn't really interest you. You may be tempted to let the person know. Instead, give yourself a learning goal, listen for a while, and then wait for the topic to change.

People expect

... that you care more about them than about the topic.
There are always new fun topics coming along.

What to do

1. **Say only one sentence at a time.**
   Watch for permission signals.

2. **Follow topic changes.**
   Don't hog a conversation or try to steer it the way you want it to go.

3. **Give permission signals when you are the listener.**
   Nods, smiles, eye contact, and small questions help the speaker to know whether or not to continue talking.

6. Repairing conversations

Many things can go wrong in a conversation. It might turn into an argument. Somebody might get offended. Someone might accidentally say something embarrassing. Someone might interrupt very rudely. Or people might just get confused.

A broken conversation is like a broken engine. It stops running smoothly. However, like an engine, a conversation can be repaired.

When a conversation breaks down, people need to fix it, sometimes right away. Otherwise, the breakdown problems will damage the relationships.

Signs of a conversation problem:

- a sudden silence, or people suddenly leaving
- people catching each other's eye, looking worried
- smiles suddenly vanishing
- someone looking angry
- someone looking hurt
- someone looking embarrassed

What to do:

- **Stop talking:** Start observing. Ask yourself: Who looks upset? Who looks worried?
- **Recall who was the last person to speak:** What did that person say? Consider how it might have affected other people in the group.
- **Watch others:** Someone might start fixing the conversation. If so, cooperate with that person. The sooner the problem is fixed, the better.

The conversation repair kit

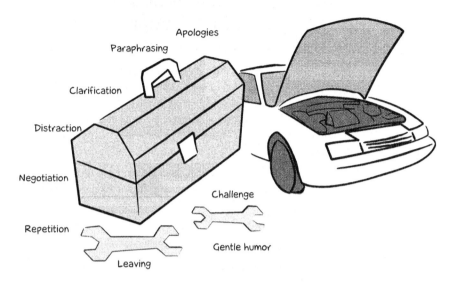

Tools in the repair kit:

- **Apologies:** Say *I'm sorry* for what you've said. Or help others say *I'm sorry* for what they said.
- **Paraphrasing:** Summarize what someone said to help clear up a misunderstanding.
- **Repetition:** Ask someone to repeat what he/she said if you aren't sure you heard it right.
- **Clarification:** Ask someone what he/she meant if you aren't sure if you understood his/her meaning.
- **Humor:** Use mild jokes to distract the conversation away from a disagreement or embarrassing moment.
- **Negotiation:** Help people work out their differences.
- **Challenge:** Gently challenge a negative comment by offering a positive opinion.
- **Distraction:** Introduce a different subject to allow people to abandon the problem and move to a safer topic.
- **Leaving:** As a last resort, if the problem doesn't get fixed and seems to be getting worse, excuse yourself and leave. If you stay, it will look as if you agree with the negative comments being made.

Everyone had been talking and laughing, and now suddenly there was an awkward silence.

Kate wondered: What had happened? Tony had been the last person to speak. He'd talked about the fossils he'd found with his cousin last week and what parts of evolution they belonged to. Then Kate remembered: several of the people present belonged to fundamentalist religions that didn't believe in evolution.

"Well, speaking of dinosaurs," she said quickly with a grin, "what do you think of that old guy that just got on our city's ball team?" (*distraction, humor*)

Her friend Liz grabbed the distraction topic. "I couldn't believe it. He's twice the age of the other players."

The church-goer friends looked more relaxed. But now Larry looked annoyed.

"That guy's my uncle," he said flatly.

Kate groaned inwardly. How many problems was this conversation going to have?

"I'm sorry, Larry," she said quickly. "I didn't mean to make fun of him. I just thought it was an unusual choice, that's all." (*apology, clarification*)

"He's a really good player, you know," Larry said defensively.

"But everyone knows that old guys aren't as strong as the young guys," Mickey said.

"Really?" Kate said quickly. "I wouldn't be so sure of that. Some of the best hitters in the league are the older players." (*challenge*)

Larry gave Kate a quick smile of thanks.

   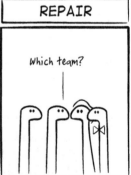

Conversation

Identify the Conversation Repairs

What happens	Type of repair
Tim gives directions to his house for the party. But he says them so fast that half the group doesn't understand. You say, "Hey, Tim, can you say that again a little more slowly?"	
Gina says angrily that she's doing more work than Lyn. Lyn looks insulted. You say, "Gina, why don't you tell us what you think we should all do as our share? And Lyn, you can explain what you've done."	
Everyone is starting to argue, ignoring all your efforts to calm things down. You excuse yourself and go find other friends.	

People expect

... that you have a sense of humor.
People like to have fun while talking.

People assume

... that you appreciate jokes and humor.
They don't understand how someone could dislike humor.

7. Having a sense of humor

Humor adds interest to a conversation. People enjoy cleverness and like to laugh. It makes them feel good. So humor is an important part of conversation

One important skill for a sense of humor is to be able to laugh at yourself. Good friends use humor to strengthen their friendship. A joke between friends has non-verbal messages buried inside it:

> "Here's a silly joke about you. I'm saying it because we are such good friends, we can joke around. Next time, you can make a funny joke about me. And we'll both have a laugh. We mean it just for fun."

> "You are I are new friends. Here's a joke to see if you have a sense of humor. I hope you do. If we can joke around together, then we can have a lot of fun."

Often when people make jokes about you, they're not expecting you to get angry. They are not laughing *at* you; they want to laugh *with* you.

They expect you to join in the joke. Together, you and the joker can share a laugh, which helps build your connections with each other. Later, it'll be someone else's turn to enjoy a joke about him/herself.

Reasons why people use humor:

- **To lighten up a conversation that is becoming too serious for the shared perspective**

"Wow. I'm so depressed now that I'm going to need to get another burger!"

"Let's propose a toast: to all the idiots who run this college!"

- **To repair a conversation breakdown or ease up a tense situation**

    "Jen, get a grip! Poor Jeff here is going to need therapy soon!"

    "Look, nobody's perfect. We all have to start admitting our faults. I would start by admitting mine... if I had any!"

- **To express an opinion in a way that will not offend people**

    "This soup could use a bit more salt. Maybe just a teaspoon.... or four.... teen. What I'm saying is that we can all be grateful that nobody's going to get high blood pressure from this soup."

Teasing

Teasing is about relationships too. People tease friends, not strangers. Teasing is like asking someone to play with words together and have some fun. People want you to respond with a funny comeback, or at least a laugh. Then the exchange is complete.

"You looked like a penguin in that suit you wore at the wedding! What a weird dude!"

"Hey, I would have looked a lot weirder wearing the wedding dress!"

Teasing is never mean. Teasing is not the same as mocking, taunting, harrassing, and bullying.

Irony

Irony is a type of humor that's based on context. It's like an optical illusion with words. There is a plain meaning based on the words and an ironic, opposite meaning based on the context. Sometimes irony is based on personal perspective: you need to think about the person saying it to pick up the double meaning.

Usually the ironic meaning is the opposite of the plain meaning. It can also be exaggerated or understated.

Often the context (place, time, circumstances, and people) provides the lens for understanding the double meaning.

People can use their voice, face, and body language ironically. The grumpy face in this cartoon is the context that gives the words the opposite meaning.

Irony can be gentle or severe depending whether the person uses a friendly, sympathetic tone or a harsh, sarcastic tone.

Sarcasm

Sarcasm is irony that includes criticism or some other kind of "bite." It's fun only when it focuses on something neutral, such as government, weather predictions, or objects. Sarcasm can be very harsh and mean when it's used to attack individuals.

Sarcasm is complex. It involves humor, criticism (helpful or mean), and witty wording. But it also includes relationships. Is the person trying to be helpful or funny? Or is the person trying to be hurtful?

Sometimes sarcasm with friends is useful. For example, you can use it to get a close friend to see when he/she is being illogical—but only if you use it gently.

Sarcasm should never be used in a group conversation to single out one person for criticism.

Types of sarcasm

Your friend says he is going to climb a hill that is obviously extremely steep and dangerous. You want to persuade your friend into being reasonable by using humor.

Here are some different types of sarcasm you can try:

- **Exaggeration:** *"Wow! What a fantastic idea! A beginner like you should have no problem scaling that cliff!"*

- **Understatement:** *"Sure, it's only a small mountain. It can't be that hard to defy gravity for 200 meters."*

- **Rhetorical question:** *"What difference could a fall of a few hundred meters have on your life anyway?"*

- **Absurdity:** *"While you're at it, why don't you swing on a vine out over the ocean and harpoon some sea bass to sell to help pay for your hospitalization?"*

What to do about sarcasm

Most people find sarcasm difficult to handle. If you do too, then you're not alone. Consider trying some of these strategies with sarcasm:

Sarcasm from a friend:

- **Stop and think:** Responding angrily will damage your relationship. Also, the friend may have made the comment to be helpful, such as to help you see that you are being illogical.

What to do

1. **Consider the intent.**
   Some sarcasm is not mean.
2. **Figure out what it means.**
   It may mean you are doing something wrong.

- **Look for the intent:** Is the friend being humorous or malicious? If humorous, then laugh.
- **Look at yourself:** Is the friend making a good point? If you did something wrong, apologize. Focus on maintaining the relationship. If you don't understand the comment, then quietly ask the friend to explain. If the person refuses to explain kindly, then he/she is not really a friend.

From a non-friend:

- **Stop and think:** If you respond angrily, then you let the sarcastic person know that he/she hurt you.
- **Look for the intent:** Some people are naturally witty and humorous. They make ironic and sarcastic comments all the time. If the comment is from a funny person, then laugh. Don't take it seriously.
- **Don't be a sponge—be a mirror:** Instead of absorbing the sarcastic comment and feeling bad, reflect it back at the sarcastic person.

  "You must be having a really bad day."

  "That sure was classy."

- **Respond with seriousness:** Take the bite out of the sarcastic comment by treating it like a regular comment.

  "Thank you. I like to dress creatively. And you look great too." (response to sarcasm about the way you dress)

- **Keep some comebacks handy:** Use a comeback, then smile and leave immediately. Don't wait for more abuse.

  "Oh, thaaaaat's nice." (sound bored)

  "You're so cool—I wish everybody could be cool like that."

  "You've obviously mistaken me for someone who cares."

  "Stop bothering me. Don't you have a life of your own?"

- **Ignore it.** If you just walk away without responding to the sarcasm, you will feel emotionally devastated, and the sarcastic person will probably feel triumphant. But it's better than saying something you regret. In the future, avoid this person.

What to do

1. **Consider the intent.**
   Laugh at sarcasm that's just meant to be witty and funny.

2. **Don't be a sponge.**
   Avoid taking the sarcastic comment too seriously. Reflect it back on the sarcastic person.

3. **Have some comebacks handy.**
   Keep them simple to avoid escalating the sarcasm.

4. **Leave.**
   Don't wait for more.

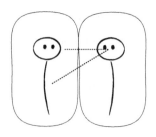

8. Personal space

Remember that people don't feel safe if other people creep into their personal health and safety zone. The same is true for conversation. You can tell when you have stepped into someone's personal space because they start backing up.

Why people need personal space in a conversation:

- **To see non-verbal communication:** People need to be able to see your body in order to read your body language. If they can't see how you're standing, moving, and gesturing, they won't get your whole message. So people stand far enough back to see your whole body at a glance.

- **To feel safe:** People like to be far enough way that they don't have to breathe someone else's breath. Strangers stand farther apart than close friends.

- **To be able to move:** People want to be able to gesture without hitting the other person. They want to feel able to leave the group when they've had enough. When people are too close, they feel caged-in.

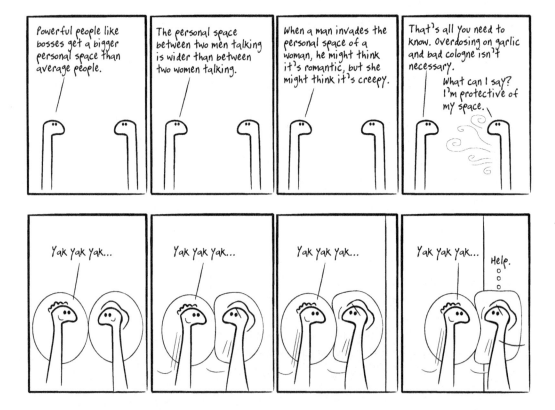

Summary

A conversation is like an engine. Each person's part of the conversation has to coordinate with everyone else's to keep the conversation going. A conversation is about

- **people:** The goal of a conversation is to learn about each other, not to lecture or make a speech.
- **equality:** Avoid being the center of a conversation. Do your share of listening and giving permission signals.
- **personal perspectives:** People think differently from each other. You can communicate with someone only if you adapt your words, topics, and ideas to the way that person thinks.
- **groups:** In group conversations, there is only a small shared perspective. Keep the conversation light, and follow the patterns of small talk.

The four unwritten rules of conversation:

- **The permission rule:** You have to get a permission signal from the listener(s) to continue talking.
- **The one-sentence rule:** You can offer only one sentence at a time. You need a permission signal to continue.
- **The no-hogging rule:** You have to let everyone participate equally in the conversation.
- **The topic-change rule:** You have to follow a topic change, even if you had more to say.

Three final points about conversation:

- **Conversations need to be repaired:** When a conversation breaks down, everyone needs to help repair it. Avoid letting a conversation problem damage relationships.
- **Conversations use humor:** Jokes, irony, and sarcasm are common in conversations. Learn to accept humor and respond to it appropriately.
- **Respect personal space:** People need space to see non-verbal communication and body language. Avoid crowding people by standing too close.

Common sense is a tricky subject, but it's not impossible to learn. Apply the skills and strategies you've learned in this book, and you'll become *commonly sensible*.

Suggested Answers to Quiz Boxes

page 10: Answers will vary. If you check all four, then you probably have a bubble mind.

page 11: Answers will vary. If you check all four, then you probably have a hummingbird mind.

page 16: If I don't signal and wait for the other lane to clear, then other drivers won't know what I'm doing (and I might cause an accident). • Cats need food and water every day. • If nobody else remembers to feed the cat, then the cat will go hungry today.

page 18: My friends expect me to share the chips with them. • She expects me to return it in good condition as soon as possible. • He expects me to keep running in the same direction so that I can catch the ball.

page 22: 4, 1, 3, 2

page 23: Answers will vary. If you check all four, then you probably get brain freezes.

page 25: Answers will vary. If you check all four, then you probably are impulsive.

page 26: Answers will vary. If you check all four, then you probably get preoccupied.

page 33: To show respect, to grieve, to support the family • Don't be noisy or boisterous. Don't crack jokes or act silly.

page 38: Sam might get really sick eating hotdogs. He might even feel sick at the thought of eating hotdogs. I shouldn't suggest it to him. • Louise will fidget, look anxious, and glance at her watch. She will be angry because I'm going to make her late. She might interrupt me and leave.

page 40: I will hang my jacket where it can air out and dry. I won't hang it in the closet because it won't dry properly and might get mildew.

page 44: 4, 1, 3, 4, 5

page 48: tax information, bank account balances, debts, financial plans • personal life, health issues

page 58: 2, 3 (or 4), 5, 4 (or 5), 5

page 60: yes, yes, yes, no

page 62: Answers will vary. Suggested answers: yes, no, yes/maybe, yes/maybe, no, yes page 64: 2, 3, 4, 5 (or 4)

page 80: Sam will catch (or kill) the beetle. He will act and do something about the problem.

page 81: Les would probably be very nervous. He would be afraid of doing something wrong. He would feel incompetent.

page 86: People will conclude that I am lazy and unhelpful.

page 88: "You take me for granted and don't respect my property. Now I don't like your borrowing my things."

page 94: no, yes, yes, no, no, yes

page 110: "This hurts me. I don't feel safe around this person. This is assault."

page 114: 4 (or 5), 2, 1, 4, 5, 1

page 128: B, C, C, C, B, B

page 131: "You don't respect me or value my time. You make me feel angry about helping you. I'm not going to drive you anywhere anymore. You can take a bus."

page 147: bad, good, bad, bad, good, good

page 157: A questioning expression. It means *Do you really think you should be doing that?* or *Does this really make sense?* or *Should we get out of here?*

page 165: You did it on purpose because you were angry. You wanted to mess it up to show that you didn't want to do the dishes.

page 195: repetition (or clarification), negotiation, leaving

CPSIA information can be obtained at www.ICGtesting.com
Printed in the USA
BVOW09s2207020815

411521BV00010B/57/P

9 780981 143958